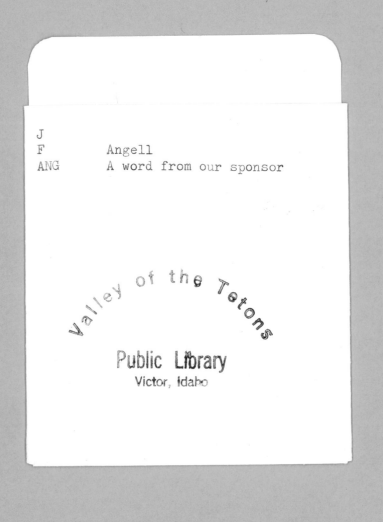

# A Word From Our Sponsor
## or
# My Friend Alfred

## DATE DUE

| | | | |
|---|---|---|---|
| FEB 23 81 | | | |
| APR 3 1981 | | | |
| JAN 29 '82 | | | |
| AUG 1 7 '89 | | | |
| JUL 31 1998 | | | |
| | | | |
| | | | |
| | | | |
| | | | |
| | | | |
| | | | |
| | | | |
| | | | |
| | | | |
| | | | |
| | | | |
| | | | |
| GAYLORD | | | PRINTED IN U.S.A. |

BRADBURY PRESS / SCARSDALE, NEW YORK

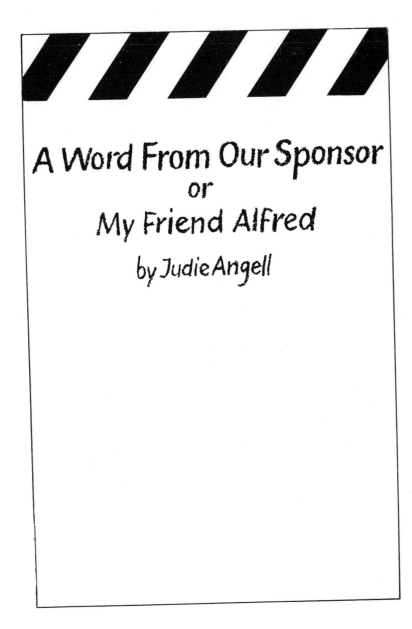

# A Word From Our Sponsor
## or
# My Friend Alfred
### by Judie Angell

Library of Congress Cataloging in Publication Data
Angell, Judie. A word from our sponsor.
Summary: When a twelve-year-old boy tries to protect consumers from a
dangerous drinking mug, he discovers he must challenge his father's advertis-
ing agency.
    [1.  Consumer protection—Fiction.     2.   Family life—Fiction.
3.  Humorous stories]     I.   Title.
PZ7.A5824Wo      [Fic]      78-25716
ISBN      0-87888-142-5

*To my son, Mark*
*with love*

# 1

Picture this: your average, ordinary Monday school morning, the kind we all know and love.

My friend, Alfred Caro—my now-famous friend Alfred—was in a bad mood. I know because he told me. The whole story, right from the beginning. He could do that because he has this scientific mind that makes him remember little details and conversations.

That morning—it was the Monday exactly two weeks ago—Gillian Tenser came down from her apartment on the fourteenth floor to Alfred's on the tenth. (Actually, Gillian lives on the thirteenth floor, but a lot of people are superstitious so most buildings just skip number thirteen on the elevator and go right from twelve to fourteen. Gillian isn't at all superstitious and she always says she lives on the thirteenth floor which sends delivery men up the wall.)

Gillian and Alfred both live in a real old building on the upper East Side of Manhattan, four blocks away from mine. Alfred says that Gillian calls for him because she always has so many books and needs help carrying them. Alfred, himself, hardly ever takes books home from school. Any book they have there, he owns a better one.

Gillian noticed Alfred's bad mood right away . . .

"You're usually a quiet boy, Alfred," she said, "but this is ridiculous! You haven't even grunted at me, and we've come down ten floors together in the slowest elevator in New York and walked two blocks!"

Alfred said, "Yeah, well . . ."

"Did you have a fight with your parents?" (Gillian's parents are divorced, so she thinks about family relationships a lot.)

"Naw, it wasn't that . . . it was what happened to Douglas." Douglas is Alfred's little brother.

"Douglas has chicken pox. So what?" Gillian asked. "I had them when I was his age, too, didn't you?"

"No. Anyway, it wasn't the chicken pox. See, because he's sick and has to stay in bed, my dad went out and bought him this toy he's been dying for. He saw it on a commercial."

"Naturally," Gillian laughed. "What toy was it?"

"It's called Muscleman. Have you seen it?"

"The doll with the wavy blond hair and the body that looks like it lifts weights every morning?"

"That's the one. Anyway, he couldn't wait to open the box, he was so excited, and then when he did, the toy table wasn't in there with the doll. You know, Muscleman's supposed to do this karate chop and break the toy table. . . ."

"Oh, yeah . . ." Gillian said.

"So I looked at the box, and down in the corner it said the toy table was supposed to be 'purchased separately.' But Dad hadn't seen that and in the commercial, it shows the whole thing together."

"So you figure that the table comes in the box," Gillian said. "Okay, so?"

"That's not the bad part," Alfred said. "Douglas pressed the button in Muscleman's neck, the one that's supposed to move his 'karate chop' arm, and guess what happened?"

"Muscleman slugged Douglas?" Gillian asked.

"No. Muscleman's head fell off."

3

Gillian shrieked with laughter.

"It's not funny, Gilly," Alfred said, laughing in spite of himself. "Really, it's not. These stupid commercials make me so mad. Little kids take them very seriously, you know. They don't watch them with the sophisticated taste that older people have. They believe every word."

"You're right," Gillian said. "Little kids believe everything they see. Especially on the tube. Wait a minute, hold these." She gave Alfred the rest of the books she was holding while she bent down to tie her sneaker. (Gillian's always got a shoelace loose or a button missing. One time she was even missing a whole sleeve, but she said the shirt was designed that way.) When she stood up, she said, "Listen, what'd your father have to say about it? He writes commercials for a living."

Alfred laughed. "He said, 'Stupid commercials.' "

They came to a light at the corner of our school. "Well, don't worry about it," Gillian told him. "There's nothing you can do about it anyway."

They headed right for the coat room, and that's where they met me, Rudy M. Sugarman, best friend of the aforementioned Alfred Caro. Alfred said, "Come on, Rudy, go get your book, we've got Science."

"Science?" I said incredulously. "*Science*? Are you kidding? Do you know what's playing on Part One of the Ten O'Clock Movie on Channel 9?"

"Aw, Rudy . . ."

"*Only* 'Buck Privates' with Abbott and Costello, that's all! I've gotta go home! I only came in to register so I wouldn't be marked absent. I'll be back," I said. I meant it, too. I love Briarfield. It's the best school I've been to so far. They really give you your *freedom* there. See, I have this disease— it's called Addiction-to-Old-Movie-itis. If *TV Guide* says that Channel 5 is showing "The Maltese Falcon" at 2:00 in the afternoon, I just have to be there to see it. I have to. I mean, it's Humphrey Bogart, for crying out loud. And at Briarfield, they don't seem to mind your cutting classes like other schools do.

So I wasn't there for the fateful Science class, conducted by R. B. Rittenhaus, who also happens to be my advisor, in which my friend Alfred Caro began to make history. But Alfred told me about it.

When he walked into the science lab, lots of the kids including Gillian were already seated on their stools and listening to R.B. on the subject of environmental control: "Some of the industrial countries have used so much mercury that it has led to contamination in many fish."

Alfred raised his hand as he slid into his seat. "That's true, Dr. Rittenhaus, especially swordfish and tuna. There was a big article on that in this month's *Our Planet* magazine." (We all call R.B. "R.B." except Alfred, who calls him "Doctor.")

R.B. nodded. "I'm glad you read that, Alfred," he said. Alfred remembers word-for-word everything that ever came out of R.B.'s mouth. "And what we're going to do today is conduct some simple experiments to test for the presence of lead and mercury salts, so that if you ever decide to test some of the foods in your home, you'll understand the procedure."

Alfred took a whole bunch of notes. And then he stayed on in the lab when the class was over to take care of the guinea pigs.

Later, Alfred went to Math, English Literature, and Music Appreciation, where they were appreciating the music of Huddie Ledbetter, the great folk artist. But he spent the rest of the day as well as after school back in the science lab, where April, his favorite guinea pig, had given birth to May, June, and November. Alfred named all the guinea pigs by his favorite months. (R.B. calls them A, B, C, and D.)

That night, Mrs. Caro got home from work first. Her name is Libby and she's really nice. She likes old movies and fast foods. Douglas was in bed, covered with chicken pox, and his regular babysitter, Doreen, was reading to him. "Did you bring me a new Muscleman?" he yelled.

"No," Mrs. Caro called back. "We decided not to get another one. It's just not a good toy. It breaks too easily. How're you feeling, honey?"

6

Douglas said, "I'm not going on to college, Mother. I'm going to New York to become a famous rock musician." Dougy speaks the language from television shows he watches and you kind of forget he's only six-and-a-half until you realize he doesn't understand a lot of what he says.

His mother said, "You're only six, Douglas. And you're already *in* New York."

Doreen said, "It's just something he heard on 'The Brady Bunch,' Mrs. Caro."

"I feel okay," Douglas said.

"Good," his mother said. "Come on out, Doreen, I'll pay you. Alfred?"

"Mmmmm?" Alfred said. He was in his room.

"Come out here a minute. Here you go, Doreen. Thanks, and see you tomorrow."

"What is it, Mom?" Alfred came out of his room with a pencil in his mouth.

"Your dad'll be home late tonight. They're shooting a new commercial. So we'll eat early, the three of us. Set the table for me?"

"Sure," Alfred said and put the pencil behind his ear. "What's the commercial?"

"I don't know, some promotional gimmick. I forget." She turned and went into the kitchen.

"What are we having?" Douglas yelled from his room.

"My specialty! Hamburgers and french fries!" his mother yelled back.

"I thought your specialty was orange chicken,"

Alfred said as he put the silverware on the kitchen table. (Alfred helps out a lot at home. It's nice. I do it, too, when I'm at *his* house.)

"It's orange chicken when I open a can of frozen orange juice," Mrs. Caro said. "Tonight I'm opening a box of frozen french fries."

She prepared supper quickly. "Come on, Douglas," she called. "You can eat with us in here!"

"No, it is my wish to be served at my bedside," Douglas called back.

"What's that from?" Mrs. Caro asked Alfred.

"I think it was a 'Star Trek' rerun he saw last night," Alfred replied.

"Douglas, get in here!"

"Okay . . ." He came in and ate with them.

When they were finished, Douglas asked, "Mom, do you have a dessert specialty?"

"Certainly do," she answered. "Pepperidge Farm marble cake. But I put my own special topping on it."

"What?"

"Cool Whip!" She laughed.

"Ahhhhh!"

"*And* . . ." his mother added, "a maraschino cherry on top."

"Maraschino cherries have Red Dye Number Two in them," Alfred said.

"What?"

"That's supposed to be a carcinogen," he explained. "It causes cancer in rats."

"*Everything* causes cancer in rats," a voice boomed, and they looked up as Alfred's father came into the kitchen. "Hi, Lib . . ."

Mr. Caro sat down at the kitchen table and rubbed his eyes. "I knew it'd be a long one," he said. "The announcer kept muffing the product's name. We did eleven takes trying to get him to say 'Choco-Rich' instead of 'Cocoa-Rich.' Once he even said 'Crock-o-rich'! Hello, boys . . . How are the pocks doing, Dougy?"

"Pox, box, stocks," Douglas said. "Want to play Candyland?"

"No, not tonight, babe, I'm completely wiped out. If I can get up off this chair, I'm going straight to bed."

"No dinner?" Alfred asked.

"No, I'm up to here with Choco-Rich. Thanks, anyway."

"Mom didn't buy me a new Muscleman," Douglas said.

"I know that, Dougy. We discussed it. But I brought something else home for you."

"What is it?" Douglas cried. "A present?"

"Uh huh. Come on."

They all went into the living room to see Douglas' present.

"A ceramic drinking mug?" Alfred asked.

"Oh, it has a picture of Sandalwood Sam on it!" Douglas said.

"Yeah, it was the promotion piece we shot today,"

Mr. Caro explained. "Nobody took it when the commercial was finished, and I thought Douglas would like it. Turn it around, Dougy."

Alfred watched as Douglas turned the mug. All around it were pictures from the "Sandalwood Sam Cartoon Hour," which is still the most popular Saturday morning kids' show. It was when I was a kid, too. And all the characters—Tumbleweed the Donkey and Sam's faithful sidekick, Buford Bodeen—were on the mug. Douglas asked to drink out of it right away.

"Okay," his father said. "Rinse it out first."

Just then, the phone rang.

"Alfred," Mr. Caro said, "please get that, and if it's for me, say I've gone to bed, which I have. Good night."

Alfred said, "Good night, hello," into the phone. It was Gillian.

"Good night, hello?" she said.

"No, I was saying good night to my father and hello to you. Hello, Gilly."

"Hello, Alfred, listen I need your help. Can I come down there?"

"What's the problem?"

"You know that science experiment we did today? Well, I don't get it. I mean, I wrote everything down just like R.B. said, but I don't understand what I wrote. Can you explain it to me?"

"Yeah, sure," Alfred said to her. "Come on down."

10

She brought down a ton of books. "I don't get why you need all this stuff," Alfred said.

"I feel the need to surround myself with other people's knowledge. Especially when I'm having trouble with something."

"Well, you won't need them," Alfred said.

Mrs. Caro came out of the kitchen. "Hi, Gilly," she said. "We're through in there, Alfred. Your turn."

"Bring just your notebook and a pencil into the kitchen, Gilly," Alfred said. "I've got to do the dishes."

Gillian put her things on the kitchen table, where Douglas was finishing milk from his Sandalwood Sam mug. "Here's my cup, Alfred," Douglas said. He put it into the sink. "Night, folks, thanks for being with us!" he sang, and left the room.

Alfred rinsed the plates, glasses, and Douglas' mug and loaded the dishwasher while Gillian read him what she had written in her notebook.

"It sounds like a story, not an experiment," Alfred told her while he rinsed the silverware. "What did you do, write it in paragraphs?"

"Well, yeah," she said.

"You don't write a scientific experiment like that. You do it in outline form, with your objective and what you're trying to prove and everything."

"Okay, you do it," she told him.

Alfred put in the soap and started the dishwasher. " Look," he said, "Your objective is to identify the presence of lead and mercury salts, right?" She nodded. "Okay, what was the first thing we did?"

"What? I can hardly hear you over the dishwasher," she yelled.

He sat down next to her at the kitchen table. "I said, what was the first thing we did in the experiment?"

"Uh . . . we put three milliliters of lead nitrate and mercury one nitrate solutions into separate test tubes."

"Good, okay," Alfred said. He handed the pencil to her. "That goes under 'Procedure.' Write it down. Now, what's Step Two?"

"Step Two is adding five milliliters of dilute hydrochloric acid to each test tube until no more precipitate was formed. Then I write what I observed, right?"

"Right," Alfred said.

"Alfred?"

"What?"

"What did I observe?"

"You observed a white precipitate, or solid. That's what's left in the tube. That's your presence of either mercury or lead."

But Gilly still didn't get it.

"See, if there was no white precipitate, then there wouldn't be any lead or mercury. That shows that one of them's there," Alfred explained. He's really good at explaining stuff. "Now, if you ever want to test something in a lab, this is the procedure you'd

12

go through, and if you found that white solid left after you added the hydrochloric acid, then you'd know there was mercury there." He looked at her notebook page. "Now when you rewrite this disorganized glop, you put the part about the white precipitate under the heading of 'Observations,' see? You've got four headings: 'Objective, Procedure, Observations, and Conclusion.' And number each thing you did underneath."

"Yeah . . ." she said.

"It's simple, Gilly, really."

"Well, when you organize it like that, I think I get it. Thanks, Alfred, you're a real friend."

Gillian wrote and Alfred watched until the dishwasher stopped.

"How many s's in 'conclusion'?" she asked.

"One." Alfred got up and opened the door to the dishwasher to let the things inside cool. He took out Douglas' mug and burned his fingers. "Jeez, these dishes are hot!"

"Alfred, they'll cool off by themselves, don't fuss over them."

"Yeah, okay," he said. He ran his hand under the cold water tap. "Hey, Gillian, look!" he cried, holding the mug up.

She glanced at it. "Cute," she said and went back to her notebook.

"No, look at the picture." He brought it over to her.

"So?" she said.

Alfred stared at the mug. "It looks . . . lighter. Like the color faded or something."

"Alfred, are you sure 'conclusion' only has one *s*? It looks funny. . . ."

"Gillian . . ."

"What?"

Alfred shoved the cup in front of her. "The color's coming off. It came off in the dishwasher. That's what happened!"

"Oh," she said, uninterested.

"Douglas shouldn't drink out of this. He shouldn't put his mouth on it. Give me a piece of your looseleaf." He ripped out a piece of paper from the back before she could get it herself. "Pencil," he said, and she handed it to him.

"DEAR DAD," he wrote. "SEE ME BEFORE YOU LEAVE FOR WORK. DOUGLAS IS NOT TO DRINK FROM HIS MUG UNTIL I TALK TO YOU. LOVE, ALFRED." He put the mug on top of the refrigerator behind a box of tea bags.

"So you really think it's dangerous?" Gillian asked, closing her book.

"Would you want to take a chance?" Alfred said.

"What's dangerous?" It was Mrs. Caro. She had pushed open the kitchen door.

"Alfred found the design on Douglas' mug faded in the dishwasher," Gillian told her. "He's worried about Dougy drinking from it."

"I want to talk to Dad about it in the morning," Alfred added.

14

"Oh, okay," his mother said, turning on the burner under the tea kettle. "What'd you do with it?"

"It's on the refrigerator. Don't give it to Doug, Mom."

"Hey, Alfred, want to walk me to the elevator?" Gillian said, gathering her things together.

"What for?" Alfred asked. "Did you forget the way?"

The only thing Alfred told me he doesn't remember about that night was Gillian's leaving and after that. His great scientific mind was at work.

# 2

■ ■ ■ ■ ■ ■

The next morning Mr. Caro knocked on Alfred's door on his way to the kitchen. Mr. Caro's first name is Creighton. Creighton Caro. I've always thought with a name like that he should've been in old movies, but he's not, he's just in advertising. Alfred and I have something in common with our fathers, and that's the fact that neither of our fathers really understands us. Alfred is very scientific, he really is, but his father doesn't care for science at all, doesn't really get how Alfred's mind works. Myself, I love old movies and old plots and old movie stars, which you'd think my father would be crazy about, since he's old, but no, not him—he just likes sports and documentaries. So both our fathers aren't interested in our hobbies, except Alfred's father seems to be more interested in *Alfred* than I think my father is interested in *me*. I *think*; I could be wrong, I have been before. But I like being around the Caros so I'm there a lot more than I'm here. Home, I mean.

Well, that Tuesday morning Mr. Caro went to check out the note Alfred had left for him the night before.

"What's wrong, son?" he asked.

"Come on in the kitchen, Dad," he said. "I don't want Dougy to hear this. He's much too young to handle another TV rip-off."

"What are you talking about?" his father asked. Alfred closed the kitchen door.

"What did you say that commercial was for?" Alfred asked. "The one the Sandalwood Sam mug was in?"

"Choco-Rich Syrup. The Allbright Foods account we got a while back." He started pouring juice for both of them. "Remember? I was excited because it was a big one for me to write. I was in charge . . . Why?"

Alfred said, "Yeah, I remember, but that commercial's been on already."

"This is a new promotion," his father explained.

"Allbright got the idea of giving away a special drinking glass or mug with every purchase of two bottles of Choco-Rich. And that's what we filmed yesterday. What's this about, anyway?"

And then Alfred socked it to him. "Because look at this mug!" he said as he took it off the refrigerator. "The color of the design faded in the dishwasher last night. I don't think Douglas should drink from it. It could be dangerous." Alfred stood there and waited for his father to do what he was supposed to do, namely jump up, grab the mug, and cry, "Oh, my God, what have we done?" or something like that, but what Mr. Caro did was rub his eyes, yawn, and say, "I'm sure it's okay, Alfred. Put the kettle on for me, will you? And a spoonful of instant in a cup?"

Alfred got a little upset then and tried to explain to his father how he felt, but he got as far as, "But—"

Mr. Caro said, "I wouldn't worry about it if I were you, son. Why don't you keep it out of the dishwasher from now on? Maybe the water's too hot for it."

Alfred said, "Listen, I don't think the color should do that on something people drink from . . ." but his father was into checking out some doughnuts or something to eat with his coffee and was barely paying attention. Which got Alfred even more upset.

"Dad, this is just like that Muscleman rip-off all

over again. Sell the product, that's all that counts, and never mind what happens when the people take it home. How can you *do* that, Dad?"

But Mr. Caro was just trying to have his breakfast in peace. "Listen, Alfred," he began, "I don't deliberately—"

"I know, I know," Alfred interrupted, "but standing up for what's right has to start with *someone*."

Well, Mr. Caro just wasn't up to changing the world on a Tuesday morning at seven o'clock, which left Alfred pretty bugged and frustrated.

"Rudy," he said when we met in the coat room at school, "wait till you hear this!"

But I was having my own problems. "Alfred," I said, "I'm in trouble!"

"We're all in trouble," Alfred said. "Do you know what happened last night?"

"Yeah . . ." I groaned. "R.B. called my parents last night. He informed them that I hold the record for the most cuts of any student in the shortest period of registration in the history of the Briarfield School!"

"Really?" Alfred said. "I didn't think they cared if you cut here."

"They care, they care. I mean, they don't mind if you skip one or two, but they know if it's more than that. And with me it's *more* than that. When I took off yesterday for 'Buck Privates,' that probably tipped it over the edge."

"Well, gee, Rudy, just don't skip anymore. For a while. You know, till it blows over. Listen, let me just tell you what's bugging *me*," he began. "Do you know how the people are getting ripped off every day? I mean, *you* and *me*. The public! Last night, my father brought home—"

"Alfred, wait. Hold it," I interrupted. "R.B. said there's a good chance I could get kicked out of here if I don't shape up. Man, I thought this was supposed to be a progressive school."

"It is, Rudy, but it's still a school." Alfred pointed to my open locker. "Look at that. Every book in there looks brand new, even the notebooks. Piled up there just like on the first day of school. You've never touched them."

"Yeah, well, gee, Alfred . . . They never tell you what chapters to read or anything like that. How should I know what to do?"

"The idea is," Alfred explained, "they introduce stuff that's supposed to stimulate your mind and then you want to learn more. You're supposed to do it on your own."

I shook my head. "No one ever stimulated my mind. It sleeps on." I sighed.

"Well, you'd better wake it up," Alfred said, "or you'll have to leave. Don't forget, Rudy, you *came* from a school that did things like tell you what chapters to read every night, right?"

"Uh huh."

20

"And what happened?"

"I flunked out because I—" and Alfred and I finished together "—*didn't like being told what to do*!"

"Right!" Alfred said.

"Anyway, that's not all," I moaned, and wound up for the pitch. "R.B. is moving my regular monthly conference up from the end of the month to the middle!"

"Why? We always have conferences at the end of the month."

"I know, but he won't give me that much time to get it together. He wants it now!"

"Wow, that's only two weeks away."

"You're telling *me*! What can I do to impress R.B. in two short, tiny, miniscule *weeks*, Alfred?"

"I don't know, I'll try to think of something," he said.

"Alfred, my best buddy, my brilliant pal, I'm counting on you," I said. "I'm *begging* you . . ."

Alfred laughed. "Okay, I'll think, I promise. But get up off your knees." We began to walk down the hall together. "How about listening to my problem now," he said.

"Hey, Alfred, I'm sorry," I said, "but can't we just put the finishing touches on mine, first? I have to plan my daily schedule. What do you think would make the best impression on R.B.?"

"Well, we have no choice. Now we have a lecture

in the auditorium," Alfred said. (At Briarfield, special programs by visiting lecturers are on the "attendance required" list.) "But it's a good one to go to, because Dr. Rittenhaus arranged it. It's on environmental protection."

"Sounds thrilling," I told him.

"Well, it should. We can use all the protection we can get. Do you know what my father brought home last night?"

But I just wasn't listening. "Hey, Alfred?" I said, nudging him.

"Hm?"

"I just thought of something that definitely stimulates my mind, but I don't think R.B. will go for it."

"What?" he asked.

"Over there. Mary Louise Bealke."

When Alfred arrived home that afternoon, the apartment was empty. He figured Doreen must have taken Douglas to the park. Dougy's pocks were dry, and he wasn't contagious anymore.

Alfred hung his jacket on the coat rack and headed for the kitchen for some guacamole dip. There in the rack by the sink was the Sandalwood Sam mug and Alfred saw immediately that it looked even lighter than before. That led him to conclude that Douglas must have drunk out of it again. "I'll be scientific about this," he told himself. "How should I procede?" He bit his lip and thought. Then, forgetting about his snack, he raced for his room.

Alfred rummaged through his desk and pulled out some litmus paper. Next he got a small black notebook from the same drawer. Too excited to sit down, he wrote standing up: *"Objective: To detect the presence of acid in the color on a ceramic mug."* Skipping a line, he wrote: *"Procedure: 1. Soak mug in a bowl of very hot water."* He put down the pen and notebook and ran into the kitchen, where he boiled water in the tea kettle. Then he filled a clear glass bowl with the boiling water and carefully placed the mug on its side in the bowl. He watched it fill with water and sink to the bottom. Soak there a bit, he thought. Let all the color mix with the water.

He went back to his room and under *"Procedure: 2,"* he wrote: *"Dip litmus paper into hot water after the mug has had time to soak."* Alfred's litmus paper was blue. If it turns pink or red, he thought, taking a little piece of it into the kitchen, there's acid in that color.

He looked at the mug through the side of the bowl. Okay, litmus paper, he thought, do your stuff. He dipped it into the hot water, held it for a few seconds, and took it out.

"Blue!" he said out loud, frowning as he examined it. "It didn't change color. It's still blue." He threw the litmus paper into the garbage bag. "Now what?" he said. "Well, first, I'd better finish this experiment, even though it did flop. Flop? What am

I saying!" His mind raced: I called this experiment a flop! It's not a flop. If there's no acid in it, then that's *good*, not bad! He walked firmly back into his room, took a very deep breath, and picked up his pen.

*"Observations:"* he wrote. *"The litmus paper remained blue. Conclusion: The color contains no acid."* Then what does it contain?

# 3

■ ■ ■ ■ ■ ■

Lead. That's what it contained. And I gave Alfred the idea right in Science.

"I tested something at home yesterday, Dr. Rittenhaus," Alfred said, and explained about the mug.

R.B. nodded. "I admire your scientific curiosity, Alfred," he said. "Did you tell your father about it?"

"I told him when the color faded. He said not to worry about it. But I didn't mention the acid test because it was negative anyway."

I decided I'd really better try to contribute and raised my hand.

"Yes, Rudy?" R.B. said, smiling at me. Encouragement.

"Maybe there's some other kind of poison in that mug," I offered.

Alfred turned and looked at me sharply. "Like what?" he asked.

But I had shot my wad. I couldn't think of anything, so I just shrugged and tried to slink back in my seat.

"No, that's a good suggestion, Rudy," R.B. said. "Does anyone have any ideas?"

And that's when Alfred got it. He hit himself on the side of his head with the palm of his hand. "Lead!" he blurted.

R.B. smiled. "Yes," he said, "or cadmium . . ."

"I should have thought of that right away. We've been testing for the presence of lead!"

"Yeah, right!" Scott Lyons put in. "I've heard of that before . . . lead in paint. But didn't they make a law about putting lead in housepaint and stuff that gets near kids?"

"Yes, Scott, there is such a law," R.B. said, "but testing never hurts. A scientist should eliminate all the possibilities before he declares something to be a fact."

Alfred left school right after Science class—something he'd surely never done before. He knew

26

no one would be home. Douglas was back in school, and both his parents would be at their respective offices.

It took him fifteen minutes to get to the apartment, grab the mug, and run back to school. The next thing was to find *me*. Third period is elective, as is fifth and seventh, and Alfred knew I could be anywhere. But good old Alfred, my friend Alfred, he just used his great scientific mind and figured it out: Let's see—Mary Louise Bealke wants to be Secretary of State, so she's probably in Government. If Mary Louise Bealke's in Government, maybe Rudy went there, too.

"What's the idea?" I asked him as he pulled me out of the class.

"Listen," he said. "I've got something in mind. It could be nothing, but it could also be a way to solve your problem and mine, too. Just don't say anything to anyone until we find out."

"What? Find out what?" I wanted to know.

"Well, remember your idea in Science this morning? You know, about there maybe being some poison in the glaze?"

"Oh. The glaze on Dougy's mug."

"Right. Well, I want to run a few tests on it, and if you help me, I'll give you credit as my assistant. That'll show Dr. Rittenhaus that you really care. You know, that you're involved in extra-credit work, outside of school. What do you think?"

That's where it began for me.

"Alfred!" I cried, feeling that cartoon light bulb click on over my head. "Suppose I do a report on this! You know, to present in front of R.B. and my parents at the conference? Wouldn't that be a knockout way to show that I'm involved, that I deserve to stay in school? How about it, what do you think?"

"Well . . ."

"I'll just write everything up as we go along! Boy, this is great, Alfred. Thanks. Thanks a lot! For this I don't mind leaving Government class."

Alfred said, "Who're you kidding? What you were studying in there wasn't Government!"

We went into the science lab, where Alfred took the mug out from his jacket.

"Okay," I said, "what do we do?"

"We find a test to detect the presence of lead oxide. I'll see what I can find, and you write."

I went over and got pencil and paper from the end of the table. "What do I write?" I asked.

"Write down 'Objective, Procedure, Observations, and Conclusions.' Write them like headings, skipping lines in between. Then we'll fill in what we did together. We've got to get it all down, Rudy. Organize it on paper, and we'll know what to do next." Then he added, "I hope." He went to the shelf of reference books next to R.B.'s desk.

"What are you boys doing?" R.B. asked. He was standing at the door.

I jumped up. "We're working on a special project, R.B.," I said.

"We didn't think you'd need the lab this period, Dr. Rittenhaus," Alfred explained. "Don't you work with the fourth graders usually?"

"Yes, but I came to get A and D," R.B. said, picking up the small cages of guinea pigs. "You may certainly carry out your experiment, Alfred." He tilted his head and looked at me. "Nice to see you here, Rudy," he said. "Just visiting?" He smiled.

"Oh, no, R.B.," I said quickly. "I'm very involved in this. This is my project, too."

"Glad to hear it," R.B. said. He nodded and headed for the door. Alfred went back to his reference material, but I didn't want to lose the opportunity to make a bigger impression on R.B., so I called out, "Uh,—R.B.?"

"Yes, Rudy?" He paused on his way out.

"What we're looking for, sir, is a simple test to detect the presence of lead oxodide in a solution. Could you tell us where to find one?" I nodded toward the books.

"Beg pardon?" R.B. said.

"*Ox*ide," Alfred whispered.

I whispered back, "Huh?"

"*Ox*ide. Not ox-o-dide," Alfred mumbled through a cough.

"Uh, lead *ox*ide," I corrected.

"Ah," R.B. said. "There's a book with a yellow

cover over there, Alfred. I believe it will be under Experiments Thirty-one through Thirty-five."

"*I'll* find it," I said, backing toward the pile of books and grinning at R.B. the whole time. But the teacher had turned and hurried out.

"Think he was impressed?" I asked.

Alfred just smiled.

"*I* was impressed, boy! I've never said words like that in my life." I lowered my voice and repeated, "I'd like a simple test for the presence of lead ox-odide, sir."

"Jeez, Rudy, it's *ox*ide, for Pete's sake," Alfred said. "Ah, here it is. 'Experiment Thirty-four: Detecting Lead and Mercury in Our Environment.' Lead, lead . . . okay . . ." Alfred read it and closed the book. "We have to soak the mug in an acid solution. Vinegar. White distilled vinegar." He looked around. "Do you see any vinegar?"

"Why don't I run down to the cafeteria and get some from them?" I said. "You check the shelves here."

"Good idea," he said, and I took off.

I had no trouble getting it. I told the dietician it was for a very important scientific experiment, and she gave me a whole bottle. Alfred was waiting with an empty bowl on the table.

"Oh, great!" he said, grabbing the bottle. "I couldn't find any." He set the mug in the bowl and poured the vinegar all around it. We both stared at it.

30

"Okay," I said. "It's sitting in vinegar. Now what?"

"It's got to sit for about twenty minutes, half an hour," Alfred said. "Then we add a few drops of potassium iodide. If lead is present, the whole solution will turn yellow."

I sighed. "We sit and stare at this for twenty minutes?" I asked.

"No. You write. Under 'Procedure,' write down about the vinegar and potassium iodide."

"How do you spell 'potassium iodide'?"

"Here," he said, handing me the book. "Page fifty-three. Copy it." He went to get the stuff, along with an eyedropper. When the time was up, he said, "Okay, Rudy, get ready. I'm doing it now. Watch!" He let three drops fall into the bowl.

"Look! It's yellow!" I yelled.

"Yeah!" Alfred breathed.

His eyes were wide.

"Pretty," Gillian said. She had been standing at the door but came in and sat down.

"Gillian, what are *you* doing in here," I grumbled at her. "We're having a private scientific conference."

"The science lab is not private," she said. "I came down to play with Lucy, Ricky, and Ethel."

"Who?" I asked.

"The new guinea pigs. The babies. Alfred, why are you staring at that bowl?"

"There's a whole lot of lead in that glaze," Alfred said quietly. "Rudy, let me finish writing this up." I handed him the paper and pencil.

"What are you guys doing, anyway? Especially you, Rudy. . . . I heard you'll be leaving us shortly. We're getting ready to decorate the Rudy Sugarman Memorial Locker, with every book untouched, exactly as you left it."

"Very funny, Gillian," I mumbled. "Anyway that's why I'm here. Alfred and I are working on a special project. One that happens to be very important, right, Alfred?"

Alfred was slowly shaking his head back and forth as he stared at the written experiment in front of him. "Gillian, this is really awful," he said. "Come here, look at this." He held the paper up for her to read.

She read it carefully and then stared at the bowl with the mug in it.

"Oh!" she said. "It turned yellow! That means there's lead in it, right?"

"It's *bright* yellow," Alfred said. "And you know what the solution is?" Gillian shook her head. "It's the glaze from Dougy's Sandalwood Sam mug!" Alfred sat back and waited for her reaction.

"Oh, wow!" she said.

"That mug is very dangerous," Alfred said. "Do you know that household poisoning has resulted from drinking water that's carried through lead pipes?"

"Really?" Gillian said.

"This is a lot more than just a school project, Rudy," Alfred said. "This is really important! This mug is going on the market soon! They already shot the commercial for it!"

"What are you going to do?" Gillian asked.

"Well, we have to stop this mug from being used by anyone," Alfred said.

"That's right!" Gillian put in.

"What do you mean, that's right?" I asked her. "This project is Alfred's and mine. Go play with Meathead, Zero, and Fat Albert!"

Gillian stood up and put her hands on her hips. "Those guinea pigs are Lucy, Ricky, and Ethel," she said.

"May, June, and November," Alfred mumbled.

"Anyway," Gillian said, still standing, "I want to help. Please, Alfred? This sounds really important."

"Gilly, I really need this to stay in school!" I told her. "To you it's just *interesting*. To *me*, it could be the saving of my life!"

"Hold it," Alfred said. "It could be the saving of a lot of lives. And I'm not kidding, either. Gilly can help, we need all the help we can get. And you'll still be able to stay in school, Rudy, once Dr. Rittenhaus reads your report. I'm going to take some solutions home. Listen, can you guys come with me after school, and we'll work on it?" he asked.

"Sure, *I* can," Gillian said. "See you guys at lunch!" and she took off.

"Listen," I whispered to Alfred. "If Gillian's in on this, can I ask Mary Louise Bealke?"

Alfred jabbed me with his elbow.

"Here's the mug," Alfred said before we even took off our coats. "Look how the design comes practically right up to the rim. See? Little kids could put their mouths right on the design and eat that glaze."

"That's true," Gillian said. "And babies, especially. They like to *chew* on their drinking cups."

"Okay," I said. "What do we do?"

"I'll show you," Alfred said.

The three of us went into Alfred's room, and Alfred took out the papers with his tests on them.

"I want us to coordinate this material and write it up again, really neatly, and tonight I'll present it to my father. When he sees how scientifically we went about this, he'll be impressed enough to do something about it. And he'll have something concrete to take to the office tomorrow."

"Alfred, if I live to be a hundred years, I'll never be able to make this up to you," I said and meant it. "No kidding, what can I do for you in return?"

Alfred looked very serious. "You know what, Rudy? We'll all be rewarded if we can save a lot of little kids from getting sick. The public is getting ripped off every day by the junk they see on the tube, and it's not fair."

"That's right," Gillian said. "If it's on TV then it ought to be *true*."

"Especially for little kids," Alfred said.

I applauded. "I'm sold," I said. I admired Alfred a whole lot for wanting to save all the little kids, but I have to admit, that right then I was mostly thinking of saving *this* little kid. Bob and Marjorie Sugarman's baby boy, Rudy.

"Let's get started," Gillian said.

We were busy discussing whether or not our headings should be written with blue or red ink, when Douglas came home with Doreen. We could hear them in the living room.

"It's a bird, it's a plane, it's yyyyy-oooowwww Soo-perman!" Dougy yelled, and there was a thud. I figured he either charged into the couch or the wall.

"How about juice and cookies?" Doreen asked him.

"Yes, please, orange juice—and in my Sandalwood Sam mug," Douglas called.

Alfred leaped up out of his chair and charged into the living room. "*No!*" he cried. Gillian and I followed.

Douglas screamed.

"Sorry, Dougy," Alfred said. "I didn't mean to scare you, I just—"

"I wasn't scared," Douglas said, narrowing his eyes, "I was angry. Do you know what happens when I get ang–ry? My muscles bulge, my clothes are too small, I grow to be seven-foot-three, I turn—"

" 'The Incredible Hulk,' " Gillian said, nodding. "Remember that program?"

"Oh, yeah," I said.

"Listen, Doug," Alfred went on, "don't drink anything out of the Sandalwood Sam mug, okay?" He looked at Doreen while he was talking. "It could be dangerous, and we want to make some tests on it first."

Douglas made his eyes into slits again. "Dan-ger-ous?" he asked, and rubbed his hands together the way the villains do on the cartoons.

"What do you mean, dangerous?" Doreen wanted to know.

"There's a glaze on that mug, and it has lead in it. So we don't want Douglas or anyone else to use it. I'm going to tell my father about it tonight."

I tapped the papers I was holding. "It's all here in our experiments," I said.

Gillian scowled at me. "You don't have to impress *Doreen*, Rudy," she said. "It's R.B. you tap your papers at."

"Gillian," I told her, "you're only the third assistant here. I outrank you, and don't you forget it."

Douglas rolled over on the rug clutching his stomach. "I'm being poisoned. . . ." he moaned. "Someone is out to poison all the children in Metropolis. . . ."

36

Doreen said, "Here, Dougy. Use the Dixie cup." They went into the kitchen, and we went back into Alfred's room.

Suddenly, Alfred jumped, literally, into the air. "Oh, my gosh!" he yelled.

Gillian and I both said, "What?"

"Oh . . . Oh . . . this is terrible!" he moaned.

"Alfred, what . . . ?" Gilly began.

"Look," he said, grabbing both our arms. "We've been worried about the design on the outside of the mug, right?"

Gillian and I nodded.

"Well, listen to this: This is a ceramic mug. It's a glaze. We saw the color fading from the outside because that's the only place there *is* color. But what if the glaze is fading from the inside, too?"

I said something like "Huh?"

"Rudy, the danger isn't only from the *outside* of the mug, it's from the *inside*, too. The metal could be going directly into the liquid inside, don't you see?"

"So even if the child doesn't bite on the design, he could still be getting lead poisoning from the fading glaze on the inside," Gillian said.

Alfred said, "Exactly. Especially from something like orange juice,—high acid!"

"But the inside is *white*," I said, still not getting it.

"Sure it's white, Rudy, but it's still a glaze. We

wouldn't know it was fading if it wasn't for the colored part on the design. White glaze fades too, see?"

"Yeah," I said. "Hey, let's test just the inside, the same way we did the outside?"

"Great idea, Rudy!" Alfred said. But I was sure it was what he had been about to say.

We filled just the inside of the mug with vinegar and repeated the test we had made in school with the potassium iodide. Yellow. Definitely yellow.

Then I got an idea. "Listen, Alfred . . ." I began. I didn't want to sound too pushy.

"What?"

"Well, I don't want to sound too pushy. . . ."

"Let's have it, Rudy," he said.

"Tonight, when you tell your father all about our tests and everything . . . ?"

"Uh huh?"

"Well, I'd like to be there," I blurted out. Of course, that meant I'd probably have to stay for dinner. . . .

"Of course that means I'll probably have to stay for dinner," I said, "since your parents get home late from work . . ."

"Hey!" he said. "Great idea! Yeah, stay for dinner, I'm sure it'll be okay."

"I'd like to be here, too," Gillian said. "It's a historic moment."

"You don't have to stay for dinner," I said to her. "You just live upstairs."

She sighed. "*I'd* never be pushy enough to invite myself for dinner," she said. "I only want to be here when Alfred talks to his father, that's all."

Alfred said, "First let's see how much we have for dinner, okay? But I think you all should be here for the presentation."

Historic it wasn't.

Mr. and Mrs. Caro arrived at approximately 6:30. They were carrying grocery bags so I figured my chances of staying for dinner were looking up.

Alfred helped them with the bags and looked inside. I'm sure he was thinking the same thing.

"Hey, you got enough in here for Rudy and Gilly to stay for supper?" he asked.

I made a face at Gillian but she didn't see me.

"Oh . . ." Mrs. Caro said, "Hmmm . . . well . . . sure, if we do the spaghetti tonight instead of tomorrow, I'll save the pork chops for tomorrow. . . ." she was talking to herself. "I'll just use the bottled sauce . . ."

"Oh, no, Mrs. Caro," Gillian said, all sweetness and light, "don't go to any trouble for *me* . . . ." She looked right at me. "I'll just run upstairs and eat and come back down."

"Why come back down?" Mrs. Caro sounded confused. She reached into her purse to pay Doreen who was on her way out.

"Because I'm being poisoned in my bed," Douglas groaned.

He threw himself against his mother's leg.

"Hi, Doug," his father said, coming out of the kitchen after he'd unpacked the groceries. "Who's poisoning you? The Evil Genie?"

"Uh . . ." Alfred butted in quickly, "we'll talk about all that later, Dougy."

"All what?" Mr. Caro asked.

"What do you think? Can they stay?" Alfred asked.

"It's no trouble. Sure they can stay," Mrs. Caro said, and she went into the kitchen.

Alfred said, "Thanks, Mom. The fact is, we have something to discuss with Dad after we eat."

"What is it, son?" his father asked.

"It'll wait until later," Alfred said. "I don't want to spoil your supper."

"Cray!" Mrs. Caro called from the kitchen. "Open this spaghetti sauce jar, please? Or would you kids rather have fish sticks?"

I thought I wouldn't mind both, but I wasn't about to push my luck. It also occurred to me that it was time I called my own parents to find out if I could stay, so I did. As I figured, they weren't upset at not seeing my bright and shiny face at dinner, but my dad did say he'd come over before 8:30 to pick me up. Gillian didn't even have to ask because her mother was working late, and she would've had to make her own dinner anyway.

All through the meal I was wondering how Alfred

was holding off telling his father about what we'd found. He did look kind of funny, though, while his father was drinking his coffee. He kept looking at the cup going up and down from his father's lips, and when it looked like his father had absolutely drained the last drop, Alfred shot up out of his seat and said, "*Now* I have to talk to you."

Mr. Caro smiled and shook his head while Alfred went into his room to get our notes.

"Take a look at these, Dad," he said, very businesslike. I wondered if I should stand or something.

"May I see, too?" Mrs. Caro asked, going to look over her husband's shoulder.

I decided it was time I participated. "Certainly," I said.

Mr. Caro examined the papers while we all watched and he handed each one to Mrs. C. as he finished with it. "You're saying that you found lead in the color from the Sandalwood Sam mug?" he asked Alfred.

"That's right, Dad. The solution turned a bright yellow. There's a high concentration of lead in it. And on the *inside*, too!"

Mrs. Caro went on reading while Mr. Caro put a hand over his eyes.

"You see?" Douglas said. "Poisoned in our beds."

Mrs. Caro looked up. "Are you saying that

Douglas could be hurt from drinking out of this mug?"

I said, "Exactly." And nodded. So they could tell I meant it.

"For heaven's sake," Mrs. Caro said. "Well, we just won't let him drink from it. Isn't that something? Coming right on top of Muscleman . . ."

"Now look, Alfred . . ." Mr. Caro rubbed his eyes. "I want you kids to know that I think it's great that you took all this trouble. . . ." he said, rifling the papers. "I really admire your initiative . . . I . . . I'm very proud of you, but—"

"But what?" Alfred asked.

Mr. Caro looked up, and I could see his eyes go from Alfred to Gillian to me and back again.

"Look, Alfred . . ." he began.

"Dad, we're all in this," Alfred said, indicating us. "We'd like to know what you're going to do about it. We think it's important, right, Rudy? Right, Gil?"

I felt a little funny, but I nodded. Gillian, too.

"I mean, that's why they stayed tonight. So we could all talk to you about it." Alfred finished.

Mr. Caro said, "Well . . ." and rubbed his eyes again.

I got up from the table. "Excuse me, Mr. Caro, Mrs. Caro," I said, "but I'd like to talk to Alfred a minute. . . ." I pushed him up out of his seat and yanked him into the kitchen. Gillian followed.

42

"Listen," I whispered to him. "I think you'd better handle this alone."

"Why?" Alfred said.

"Shh. Because I get the feeling your father doesn't want to talk about it in front of us. I mean, you know—"

"Rudy's right," Gillian said (first time she'd ever said *that*). "After all, it is his business, you know."

"Yeah," I said. "and besides, if he's angry or anything, I don't want to overstay my welcome."

Alfred thought about it. "But your father won't be here until eight-thirty. . . ."

"It's okay," I told him. "I'll hang around the lobby or something. It won't be that long."

"You can come upstairs with me," Gillian offered. "And then meet your father in the lobby when he's supposed to be here."

"Can we watch TV?" I asked.

She said okay.

So that's what I did.

# 4

■ ■ ■ ■ ■ ■

I decided it would be better not to call Alfred at home that night, so I was waiting for him on the steps of the school the next morning.

"Well?" I said, getting up as he approached with Gillian.

"Well, I told him and my mother that it wasn't just Douglas I was worried about, it was all those other little kids who buy Choco-Rich Syrup and get those mugs. I told him that we were lucky we found out it was poisoned, but what about all those other kids who watch that commercial and—"

I sighed. "I know, Alfred, but what happened?"

"Well, it ended that Dad'll write a memo to the account executive, Bud Diedrickson. *I* thought he should go directly to Mr. Krebs, the Chairman of the Board, but he said everything goes through the proper channels, or something like that." (Mr. Caro works for an advertising agency called Ditmar-Krebs-Patten, Inc., and Mr. Gregory Krebs was the nephew of the founder. I knew that because Alfred sometimes does imitations of him after he's been at the Caros' for dinner. Bud Diedrickson I never heard of.)

"What's an account executive?" I asked. "Will he do something by the time my conference comes up, do you think?"

"Sure," Alfred said confidently. "He's the guy who works directly with the client. Allbright Foods, who makes the syrup."

"Great." I said. "Listen, I'd better have a copy of the experiment notes."

"You bet," Alfred said. "I'll have them back tonight."

"What do you say we go to Art today?" I asked as we went into the building.

Alfred and Gillian both said, "*Art*?"

"*You*?" Gillian added.

"Now just wait a minute," I said. "It so happens I have a very terrific aesthetic sense. I am a true appreciator of culture. The more you get to know me, the more my true nature will—"

"What are they doing in Art, Rudy?" Gillian asked suspiciously.

"They're beginning sculpturing," I answered, "in soft clay."

"And *what* are they sculpting?" Gillian asked.

"A soft model!"

"—Mary Louise Bealke!" We all said together, and broke up.

I think I have a pretty good imagination. I enjoy my imagination. I mean, if I'm bored with worrying about staying in school or if there's no one around who captures my total attention like Mary Louise, then I can just make stuff up. My father, though, doesn't call it "imagination," he calls it *stop lying around there doing nothing*. But *I* know it for what it really is.

I imagined a lot, the rest of that Thursday. After Alfred told me about how his father was going to have it out with the Allbright account executive, a whole big deal because of what three kids did on their own—it was too good not to make a movie out of. I did it in my head. First I cast it with real actors, but then I decided that Alfred, Gillian, and I could play *ourselves* in my movie. I could just see it up there on the screen. . . . A closeup of a kids' mug on a TV screen, with an announcer's voice-over saying, ". . . And now, a word from our sponsor," the way they do, and that'd be the title of my movie: "A Word from Our Sponsor"—terrific, I thought, and then the camera pulls back to reveal Alfred: poised, watching, like the great Guardian Angel of Consumers.

And then, in the movie in my head, I pictured these great chase scenes, you know, where Alfred and I and Gillian are rushing through the streets, in time to stop production on the mugs before the kids run out to buy them, or rushing into the TV studio before the commercial goes on, and everyone praises us and calls us the heroes of the country. . . . Then I had the President, playing himself, decorating us on the steps of City Hall as the picture fades out, and the credits roll.

Well, that's not what happened. What happened turned out a little different from my imagination-movie, but before it got better, it got worse.

Alfred had to wait until his father came home from work that Thursday night, which didn't happen until 9:30. By that time, he was really keyed up. He had paced the living-room floor until his mother told him he was probably eroding the ceiling of the people who lived downstairs. He played his records but didn't hear one song. So when Mr. Caro actually walked through the door, Alfred almost pounced on him.

"Dad, I've been waiting and waiting. What happened with the memo and the account executive, Mr. Diedrickson?" Alfred said in a rush.

"I'd like to hear, too," Mrs. Caro said.

"Well . . . son . . . these things take a little while, you know . . .?" Mr. C. began. Now, if you've been a kid long enough, you know that every time a grownup starts a conversation with "These things take a little while," you might as well head for your room, because it's going to be twelve Christmases before you see that ten-speed bike you wanted or you take that trip to Disneyland or you single-handedly change the history of the world.

But Alfred didn't head for his room. "What do you mean? You sent the memo, didn't you?" he asked.

"Yes, absolutely. In fact, I brought you a carbon." Mr. Caro opened his briefcase. "And here are your notes back, too."

Alfred looked at the paper on top.

MEMO
TO B. DIEDRICKSON FROM C. CARO
RE: CHOCO-RICH PROMOTION
B.D.: Attached are notes from experiments performed on our Sandalwood Sam promotion piece for C-R. It seems that the glaze used appears to contain a concentration of lead in its base which might be dangerous and bears looking into. C.C.

"Dad!" Alfred wailed. "Look at these words—

'seems' . . . 'appears' . . . 'might be dangerous'!
Why did you make it sound so wishy-washy?"

Well, then Mr. Caro explained about how he was
kind of on the spot. For one thing it was his own
twelve-year-old son who made the tests (which
made Alfred's knuckles turn white) and how hard
he, Mr. C., had worked to get where he was at
Ditmar-Krebs and how his mother worked so he and
Douglas could have good educations and all that
stuff, but Alfred didn't get the connections.

"I appreciate that, Dad, I do. But I don't see what
that has to do with your pointing out something
that's not good for people," he said.

And Mr. Caro said, "Look, Alfred, I'm really
torn. This company who manufactured the mug,
they've been in business a long time, they've got an
excellent reputation. You're my son and I respect
your mind, your idealism and your enthusiasm, but
Alfred, you're twelve years old. . . ."

"Dad," Alfred interrupted, "there's lead in that
mug. It's got nothing to do with how old I am."

Mr. C. sighed. "All right. I've done what I could.
The account executive is the man to deal with it, and
he's been notified. There are channels, you do understand that, don't you?"

So there they were.

The best thing Alfred and I and Gillian could hope
for was some fast action on the part of this Mr.
Diedrickson when he got the memo. But when Alfred told us the story the next day at school, I must

admit, I wasn't very encouraged. I eliminated the President's decoration and the tickertape parade from the movie in my head.

# 5

■ ■ ■ ■ ■ ■

"I just want to know what you guys think I should do now," Alfred said. He had called a "lunch meeting" of the three of us to discuss the problem.

"I guess you just have to wait to see if Mr. Diedrickson answers your father's memo." Gillian shrugged. "What else can you do?"

"Maybe you can force the issue a little," I suggested. "I mean, I don't want you to think I'm worried because my conference is now only a week-and-a-half away or anything. . . ."

"Rudy, you're only thinking about yourself," Gillian snapped at me.

"No, I'm thinking about the poor little kid-consumers, too," I said and tried to.

"I might just go over there after school today," Alfred said.

"Where?" Gillian asked.

"To the office. Over to Ditmar-Krebs. Do you think it could do any good?"

I sighed. "I don't think you can lose anything," I told him. "It's worth a try. But honestly, does it *ever* do any good when you push adults? Every time I nag my mom or dad, they just dig their heels in, and I end up with nothing."

"Sometimes I can wear mine down by nagging," Gillian said thoughtfully, "but of course, my parents don't live together so maybe they get worn down out of guilt over me."

"I don't usually nag too much," Alfred decided.

"Oh, good," I said, "then it'll be a new experience for your father. He just might listen. Can I go with you?"

"Oh, me too?" Gillian cried.

"No, I'll go alone. Otherwise it'd look like a kid invasion. And this is too important to seem like just a kids' game."

"Well, plan a little strategy," I warned him, being an old hand at parent war. "Don't barge right in with it, kind of sneak up on it slowly so you take him by surprise. If you come on too strong, he'll just get defensive, and you'll blow it."

Alfred said, "I'll just see how it goes. . . ."

"Take it from me, I've been through this kind of thing a lot. By the way, do you know what you'll be missing by going downtown today?" I asked him.

Gillian said, "A movie, I bet,"

" 'Casablanca,' " I said. "Not just 'a *movie*.' It's with Humphrey Bogart and Ingrid Bergman! It's a classic! 'A *movie*!' Gillian, you hurt me!"

"Listen, Rudy, instead of 'Casablanca,' copy these experiments we made." Alfred took some papers out of his notebook. "Then you'll have your own copy in your own handwriting to show Dr. Rittenhaus. You know, for your report."

I took them. And I copied them. During the commercials.

Alfred always said that when he walked through the halls of Ditmar-Krebs-Patten, he was reminded of a TV-version of a space station. The whole place seemed like it was not of this world. Everything is white. And chrome. And glass. And plastic. The only things that have color are the lucite boxes along the walls, each containing a true-to-life photograph of one of the agency's products.

Flash! A bright red-and-yellow apple, used to make *Ma Hoener's Applesauce*. Flash! A little Dutch girl with blond braids, holding up a can of

*Blast Disinfectant.* Flash! A photo of a German shepherd, running for his can of *N-R-G Dog Food.*

As Alfred neared the receptionist's desk, a man bumped into him.

"Oh. Sorry. Didn't see you," the man said. He fumbled around in his breast pocket. "Have on the wrong glasses." The man straightened up and glared at Alfred. "Who are you, son?" he asked. "If you're here for casting, you're on the wrong floor."

Alfred shook his head. He recognized Gregory Krebs, the head of the agency, who obviously didn't remember *him.* "No, Mr. Krebs, I'm not here for casting," Alfred said politely. "I'm Alfred Caro."

Mr. Krebs looked blank. He must have thought that Alfred was there to audition for a television commercial.

"Caro. My father is—"

"Ah! Caro. Yes. Well . . ." he brushed himself off. "Nice to see you." And he turned away.

"Mr. Krebs?" Alfred called.

"Yes?"

"I . . . I'm—" Thoughts raced through Alfred's mind: Could he say something to Mr. Krebs? *Should* he? Would his father be mad if he did? Yes! Alfred decided to wait. "Uh, nice to see you, too, Mr. Krebs," he said. He got a blank look in return, and headed on toward the receptionist.

She glared at Alfred as if he were a bug who had just crawled up her arm.

"Casting is on the third floor," she said and continued to lick envelopes.

"I'd like to see my father, please," Alfred said. "Creighton Caro?"

The receptionist stopped licking. "Oh. Sorry." She turned to her intercom. "Is he expecting you?" she asked.

Alfred cleared his throat. "No, but if he's not too busy . . ."

"One moment." She pressed a button on the machine. "Mr. Caro, your son is here. . . . Your *son*. Yes, sir." She whirled back to Alfred. "You may go right in," she said and pointed toward his father's door.

Mr. Caro had the door open before Alfred could reach it. He put both hands on Alfred's shoulders. "What is it, something wrong at home?" he asked anxiously.

"Oh, no, nothing like that. I just . . . happened to be in the neighborhood and thought I'd drop in."

Mr. Caro smiled and led Alfred into his small office. He took books off a chair and motioned Alfred to sit. "Just a little visit?" he asked and walked around to his own chair.

"Yeah," Alfred said. "Just . . . wanted to say hello."

"Hello," his father said. "How was school? Glad you've got a weekend coming up?"

"School was okay. Yeah, weekends are nice."

There was a pause.

"Well, son, I'm glad we had this little chat," Mr. Caro said and they smiled at each other. "I'm always happy to see you, of course, but I am very busy. . . . Is there anything in particular you wanted?"

Alfred stood up. "Oh, no, no! Just . . . visiting. Well . . . 'bye, Dad."

"I'd like to take you down and buy you a soda, but I've wasted an entire day here. . . ." He waved his arm toward two wastebaskets both filled with crumpled white and pink papers. ". . . and I've got to come up with something before I leave tonight."

"I understand, Dad, really. . . ." Alfred said and backed toward the door. "Oh. Say. Dad."

"Mmmmmm?"

"As long as I'm here . . ."

"Yes?"

"I just thought I'd ask if you—"

"No, Alfred, I haven't heard anything."

Alfred coughed. "I just ran into Mr. Krebs—"

"Where?" his father asked sharply.

"Outside. In the hall. That is, he ran into *me*."

Mr. Caro put his hand up to his forehead. "Alfred . . . you *didn't* . . . you didn't say anything to *him*, did you?"

"Oh, no, Dad . . ."

His father sighed. "Good. Alfred. Someone will be looking into it, all right?"

"I guess so . . ."

"There are a lot of memos, ideas, suggestions, and orders flying around here, son," Mr. Caro said, "and all of them are marked *urgent*. Now just don't expect immediate results, okay?"

"I'll try," Alfred said.

That night the Caros' phone rang, just as they were throwing dinner together. Mr. Caro answered it.

"Alfred!" he called. "It's for you!"

"Hi, it's me, Gillian," she said before Alfred could say hello. "Your *father* answered."

"Yeah, well, he sometimes does that," Alfred said.

"No, but I mean . . . it threw me off guard. I was calling to ask what happened today. At the office."

"Nothing."

"Nothing?"

"Not really. I can't—"

"You can't talk," she said for him. "He's right there."

"Yeah."

"Well, look. Nothing can happen over the weekend, right? He's not going to the office tomorrow or anything, is he?"

"No," Alfred said. "Not that I know of."

"Okay, as long as there's nothing we can do, I had this idea. Tomorrow's my day with my father. We're going to the Natural History museum and maybe the Planetarium. Why don't you come with us?"

"Aw, gee, Gilly, I don't know . . ." But he didn't want to stay home without any plans—he'd drive himself and everyone else crazy. "Did you say the Natural History?" he asked.

"Uh huh," she said. "It was my idea."

"Well . . . okay, maybe I will. What time?"

"Eleven," she said. "So he can take us out to lunch. I'll come down and ring your doorbell."

"Eleven," Alfred said. "Okay."

# 6

■ ■ ■ ■ ■ ■

Saturday morning, I got up fairly early, for me, 9:00, to check out the Early Bird Movie. Usually, the Early Bird Movie on Saturday morning is just what early birds deserve—a worm—but I always check it out just to make sure I'm not missing anything good. So there I was, flipping channels, when suddenly I saw it! Just the way it appeared in my imaginary movie: a closeup of the Sandalwood Sam mug, in a TV commercial. Only this was live. And in person. Not to mention living color.

It was sitting on a rotating spindle, one of those things that turns the product around so you can see all angles of it. And right to the side of it were two large bottles of Choco-Rich Syrup, tied together with a bright red ribbon. It was a commercial for the "Sandalwood Sam Cartoon Hour."

I saw all this while I was dialing Alfred's apartment. How I managed to get through without getting a wrong number, I don't know, but I got hold of Alfred as the announcer was saying: "So buy two, and get this *twelve-ounce mug* with pictures of your good friends *Sandalwood Sam*, his donkey *Tumbleweed*, and *Buford Bodeen . . .*"

". . . his faithful sidekick," I finished.

Alfred said, "What?"

"Is Douglas watching the 'Sandalwood Sam Cartoon hour'?" I asked Alfred.

"I don't know. Why? Say, isn't this kind of early for you, Rudy?"

"Listen, Alfred, I just saw a commercial for the mug!" I said.

"*What*?"

"The mug! Your father's commercial! They just did it on the 'Sandalwood Sam Cartoon Hour'!"

Alfred said, "Hold on." He put the phone down (I heard it smash the table) and went to turn on their television set. I stayed there with the phone next to

60

my ear, watching, too. Finally, it came on again. The same commercial, the same closeup. No one came back to the phone but in the background I could hear a pained shriek. One of the better ones I've heard. It went "*Aaarrrrgh!*" It really did. Just like they say in the comics. The next thing I heard was Alfred, putting the scream into an actual word: "*Da-ad!*" His father must have mumbled something like, "What?" (I couldn't hear) and then Alfred yelled, "They put your commercial on! It was *on!* That means people could go right out and buy that mug today!" Then Mr. Caro said something else I couldn't hear, and Alfred said, "Well, they did, so what are you going to do *now?*"

MR. CARO. Mumble.

ALFRED. No, you *can't* go back to bed! This isn't something you can just pass off!

MR. CARO. Mumble, mumble, mumble.

ALFRED. I think you should call Mr. Krebs right now. Tell him, Dad, it'll make a special impression if you call on a Saturday. Dad, you have to stop those commercials!

MR. CARO. Mumble, mumble, mumble, mumble, not—call—Gregory—Krebs—at—home. Period. Besides, I told you—things must go through the proper channels.

Then there was this long pause. I was sure that Alfred had forgotten I was hanging on the phone so I started to yell into it. You know how sometimes the phone makes noises and crackles, and that's how you know you've left it off the hook? Well, either Alfred heard me or he remembered by himself, but he did come back to the phone.

"Sorry, Rudy. Did you hear that?"

"I heard *you*," I told him. "I guess your father isn't as excited as we are, huh?"

Alfred said, "You could put it that way."

"What now?" I asked. He told me about Gillian's invitation to join her and her father for a visit to the Natural History museum.

"I think you should come, too," he said. "That way we can all be together and decide what to do. Because something has to be done, Rudy."

"I know," I said. "Gillian might get mad, though. She didn't invite me."

"She won't get mad, why should she? We're all doing this together. Meet me here at ten-fifteen, and we'll go up to Gillian's together," he said.

At 10:20 we were knocking on Gillian's door. Mrs. Tenser, Gillian's mother, answered it. She was wearing a pair of large flannel pajamas and had big floppy slippers on her feet.

"Oh, it's you, Alfred, hi," she said and yawned. "I thought Gilly was coming down to *your* place."

"She was, but I have to talk to her. This is Rudy Sugarman."

"Hi," I said.

"Hi, Rudy. I think we must have met before . . ." she said. We had. Couple of times at Alfred's apartment and at school Parent Days.

"Where's Gillian?" Alfred asked as we stepped inside.

Mrs. Tenser stretched and rubbed the back of her neck. "I just got up," she said. "Sorry for the mess around here." She turned toward a closed door. "Gil?" she called.

"What?" from behind the door.

"Alfred and Rudy are here." Mrs. Tenser left us standing there and headed down the hall, slippers flopping.

"Alfred and *who*?" The door flew open, and she came out. She had on jeans and a pajama top. "What are *you* doing here?" she said to me.

"Gillian, you're so cordial," I said.

"I asked Rudy to come with me," Alfred told her, "because something happened this morning that we all need to talk about. That's why I came up here instead of waiting for you to call for me."

"What happened?" she asked.

"*The commercial was on*!" Alfred said.

"What commercial?"

"The mug commercial!" he shouted. "The Sandalwood Sam mug commercial was on this morning. Rudy saw it and called me."

"No kidding?"

"No kidding."

"Well . . . what did your father say?" Gillian asked.

"Nothing. He said the same thing he's been saying all along. 'I can't do anything *now*.' He just doesn't seem to understand how important this whole thing is!"

Gillian moved toward her room. "Look," she said. "I'll finish dressing, and we'll go meet my father. Maybe he'll have some ideas."

We were out on the street heading for the bus stop, when Gillian turned to Alfred.

"Do you remember my father?" she asked him.

He shrugged. "I think so. I haven't seen him . . . gee, since your parents split up, I guess. How long is that?"

"Two years," she told him. "Well . . . he's changed. I just thought maybe I should explain him to you."

"*Explain* him?"

"Mmmm. See, when my parents broke up, they both got a bad case of the guilts. My mother got over it. But my father still has it, probably because he doesn't see that much of me except on weekends."

Alfred said, "The 'guilts'?"

"Oh, yeah, you know, like my life would be wrecked forever, and it was all *their* fault for getting divorced. You know. It's a classic story."

"It is?"

"Oh, yes, that's what the shrink they took me to said."

"Well . . . it *didn't* wreck your life forever," Alfred told her.

"Of *course* it did," Gillian said as we reached the stop for the crosstown bus. "But I got over it. Put away your money, I invited *you*."

I said, "Gee, thanks, Gilly."

She scowled at me. "I didn't invite *you*," she said.

Alfred looked at me sheepishly and slipped me the change he had taken out of his pocket for himself. I took it.

"Anyway," Gillian went on, "I just wanted to explain about my father so when you see him fawn all over me you'll understand."

Mr. Tenser lived in an apartment-hotel on the West Side of Manhattan, fairly close to the museum. He was waiting in his lobby when we arrived. He was a small man with curly brown hair and horn-rimmed glasses. He had on a trench coat and a tweed hat. Gillian didn't look a thing like him.

He gave her an enormous hug.

"See?" Gillian mouthed behind his back to us.

"I brought Alfred Caro, Daddy," she said out loud.

"Oh, hello, Alfred. Aren't you the boy from downstairs?" Mr. Tenser said.

65

"Yes," Alfred said and turned to introduce me.

But Mr. Tenser went on. "Of course! Your mother recommended Briarfield for my little Gilly." His little Gilly made a face. "Well, we're very grateful. Where would you both like to go for lunch?"

I was beginning to feel like The Invisible Man, when Alfred finally dragged me into the scene. "Mr. Tenser, Rudy here's with us . . . Rudy Sugarman, Gilly's and my friend?"

"Oh, pleased to meet you, Rudy," Mr. Tenser said, holding out his hand. "Any friend of Gilly's is a friend of mine!"

I watched Gillian roll her eyes while I said, "Yes, sir."

We ate in a pancake house on 83rd and Broadway. Mr. Tenser kept asking Gillian if she had enough, if she wanted more, if she were cold, hot, happy, sad. She answered everything, but kept looking at us as if to say, Do you get what I meant before? *I* got it, but I could tell Alfred's mind was wandering. He didn't seem to be paying much attention to the Tensers' conversation until Gillian said, "Alfred, tell Daddy about the mug," and it was as if she had taken the logs off the dam. Alfred told him the whole thing, with a few inserts from me and Gilly, and he didn't stop until the story was finished, right up until that morning's commercial.

"Quite a story," Mr. Tenser said, wiping his mouth with a napkin. "You're quite a boy."

"I helped," Gillian said.

"Me, too," I said.

"Yes, I know," Mr. Tenser said. "Well, what happens now?"

"We were wondering if you'd have any ideas," Gillian said.

We stood up, ready to walk to the museum. "Gee, kids, I don't know," Mr. Tenser said, putting a tip for the waitress on the table. "It's hard, when you're a kid . . . you don't have too much clout."

"What's clout?" Gillian asked.

"Power," her father said, holding the restaurant door open for us. "Ability to carry things out because people listen to you."

"You're right," Alfred said. "Kids have no clout. But I'm not giving up, Mr. Tenser. I'm going to work on my father, and I may just have to go see Mr. Diedrickson or Mr. Krebs myself."

We began to walk east toward Central Park and the museum. "Well, you know, you can always call Ralph Nader," Mr. Tenser said, "or someone like that."

Alfred stopped walking. "Ralph Nader," he said to himself, but I heard him.

"What?" Gillian asked.

"Ralph Nader. The consumer guy," Alfred said.

"Oh, yeah. We talked about him in Social Studies," Gillian said. "He's the one who finds things wrong with products and tells the Government, right?"

"Somebody like *that* has clout," Alfred said.

The Museum of Natural History is Alfred's favorite museum, but he hardly noticed a thing in it that afternoon. His mind was racing as we walked past the dinosaur, the Eskimo village, the mammoth whale. But he tried to look as if he were studying each exhibit, and Gillian and her father didn't notice how far away he really was. I could tell, though. I mean, you can tell about your best friend most of the time.

He was thinking so fast it was like one idea was beginning before another one was completed. Ralph Nader . . . Maybe we haven't made ourselves clear enough. . . . Maybe Dad thinks I'm just a nagging kid. . . . Maybe we should find a new way to talk about it. . . . Maybe we should . . . No, that's no good. . . . Maybe we should say . . . Maybe we should do . . .

"Alfred! You almost walked into that lady!" Gillian grabbed his sleeve and pulled him toward her. "Would you look at the *bones* on that brontosaurus!"

Alfred looked at the bones but he was thinking: Ralph Nader. He didn't even tell Gillian it was a tyrannosaur.

# 7

∎ ∎ ∎ ∎ ∎ ∎

On Sunday, Alfred drove his parents out of the apartment. At least that's what he said when he called me up.

"I nagged them too much," he said.

"Alfred, there's nagging, and there's nagging. If you do it right, they don't even know they're being nagged."

"I just can't stand it, Rudy," he said. "Today's

69

one more day that kids could be buying themselves lead poisoning. I just can't stand that no one is doing anything."

"Well, tomorrow's Monday," I said. "Your father'll say something tomorrow, won't he?"

"Well, yeah, he said first thing Monday. And he really better say something, Rudy, because if he doesn't, then *we'll* have to do something. Man, he's just got to!"

"Yeah," I said, "I'm sure he will. The thing is, it's almost conference time. And I've got to have a socko-boffo sure-thing can't-fail knockout thing to show off by the time *Bob and Marjorie Sugarman Meet R. B. Rittenhaus*. Boy, is *that* a horror movie title!"

Alfred laughed. "Okay, tell you what: suppose we give him tomorrow and Tuesday. *Some*thing ought to happen in two whole days, right?"

"Oh, sure," I said, crossing my fingers. "*Some*-thing will happen."

# 8

■ ■ ■ ■ ■ ■

This is Alfred's version of Monday:

6:35 P.M.: "Dad?"

"Alfred . . ."

"I wanted to call you at the office today. You know . . . but I figured you'd just get mad."

"You figured right. But I'm mad anyway."

"Why?"

"I went up to see Mr. Diedrickson."

"You did?"

"Yes, I did, and he was in conference. I left a message for him to get back to me as soon as possible but I didn't hear from him all day. So just before I came home I left a much stronger memo with his secretary."

"Well, how about going right to Mr. Krebs?"

"Alfred, things just aren't done that way. You don't understand."

"Dad, you've got to do something more *tomorrow*! Please!"

"Why tomorrow?"

"You just have to, that's all!"

# 9

■ ■ ■ ■ ■ ■

And this is Alfred's version of Tuesday:

7:15 P.M.: "Dad . . . what happened?"

"Son, Bud Diedrickson was out of the office all day. I talked to some others in the Creative Department, but Diedrickson is the guy to see."

"*Jeez*, Dad!"

"Now, look, I have a meeting with him tomorrow afternoon. It's all set, and I'm going to talk to him, in person, face-to-face, about this whole thing."

"Dad, I'm sorry, but your two days are up."

"Alfred, you sound like a telephone operator! What 'two days'?"

"There's no more time! Douglas saw that commercial again! This afternoon! We just can't wait anymore, Dad!"

"Wait till tomorrow night, Alfred. It'll be taken care of tomorrow."

"Okay. Okay. What's one more day of poisoned children!"

"Now, just a minute, young man. Are you accusing me of poisoning *children*? I'm not going to stand here, in my own house, and have my own son—Go to your *room*, Alfred!"

"Awwwwww, *jeez*!"

# *10*

■ ■ ■ ■ ■ ■

The next day was Wednesday, and my conference was just six days away. Alfred and I were both going slightly bonkers so we decided to spend the afternoon together after school to commiserate—Alfred's description. Mine was "flip out." I wanted to wangle another dinner invitation so I could be with Alfred when his father got home, but Mrs. Caro took the wangling out of my hands.

"Want to stay for dinner, Rudy? I'll call Cray and have him bring home a pizza," she said, sticking her head into Alfred's room.

"Great, Mrs. C.," I said. "Just great."

"Okay." She was gone, and I suddenly jumped up and ran after her.

"Mrs. C.?"

"What?"

"No anchovies!" I called.

"Okay."

"Just mushroom, pepperoni, sausage, and double cheese."

"Okay."

"No, wait, forget the mushroom."

"Okay."

"Oh, and listen," I called, remembering my manners, "it's okay with me if you want to leave off anything else . . . I mean, it's your pizza. . . ."

"O-*kay*, Rudy," she called back, and I heard a small laugh.

I slipped back into Alfred's room. He was sitting on his bed, frowning at me.

"What's the matter?" I asked.

"I *like* anchovies," he said.

"Oh, hey, pal, I'll just—" I started to tell him I'd fix it with his mother before she called, but he held up his hand.

"It's all right," he said. "I probably won't be able to eat anything anyway."

76

At 7:05 we heard Mr. Caro's key in the lock. We were all in the kitchen, except Dougy, who was in the den watching television.

"Now, Alfred," his mother said warningly, "please don't pounce on your father the minute he steps in here. . . ."

We heard the door open, then a thud, which must have been Mr. C.'s briefcase hitting the floor. Then the kitchen door swung open, and he came in.

"Alfred," he nodded at his son, and then at me. "Lib?" he kissed his wife. He handed her two pizza boxes, and she got the pies into the oven to reheat.

"Dad?" from Alfred.

"Cray." A smile from Mrs. C.

"Mr. C.?" I threw in.

"Dad-deeee!" A squeal from Douglas who burst in and ran to his father. "Gotta go back! Batman's gonna get killed this time for sure! The Joker's got him tied up and a great big rabbit's going to jump out of a hat and eat him and Robin up like carrots!"

"He'll get saved, Dougy, don't worry," Alfred called as Douglas bounced out of the kitchen.

"No, he won't!" Douglas called back.

Alfred looked at me, I looked at him.

"I'm going to fix myself a drink," Mr. Caro said.

Alfred whispered, "I'll wait three minutes. Then I'll go ask him."

I nodded, and we both just stood there, looking at Alfred's watch and checking out the second hand going around. When it hit the twelve for the third time, Alfred made for the kitchen door with me following.

Trying to be super casual, Alfred began with: "Say, Dad, just thought I'd ask what happened at the meeting with Mr. Diedrickson."

"There wasn't any meeting," Mr. C. answered.

"What?"

"Bud called me around four. You want it word for word?"

"Word for word," Alfred said.

" 'What are these blasted memos and calls, Cray?' he said. I said, 'I think the Sandalwood Sam promotion piece should be re-examined, Bud. There's evidence of lead in the glaze. You saw the notes of the tests that were performed on it.' He said, 'Where'd you get those tests? Who did them?' I said, 'My son, Alfred.' He said, '*Who*?' I said, 'My son, Alfred.' He said, 'Caro, is this a gag?' I said, 'It's no gag.' He said, 'Caro, there are decals and silkscreen and glaze on nine million glasses and cups and mugs in this city. The imported ones are checked all the time, and there are specific laws about the ones made here. Besides, do you know what's riding on this? Tell your kid to use his chemistry set on stink bombs, like I made when I was a kid!' "

Alfred looked at me and shrugged. I knew how he felt . . . helpless.

"I tried, Alfred," his father said.

"I know. Now it has to be our turn to try." Alfred clapped a hand on my shoulder.

"Our?" Mr. C. asked.

Alfred cleared his throat. "Yeah. Rudy's and mine. And Gillian's." He still had his hand on my shoulder, and I could feel his fingernails dig in when Mr. C. raised his voice.

"Now look here," his father said, putting his glass down on the table, "you and your friends stay away from Ditmar, and you stay away from Mr. Diedrickson and Mr. Krebs. I mean it."

"We won't go near either one," Alfred said. "Right, Rudy?"

"Uh, yeah," I said quietly. One thing that's very bad is to butt into another person's family argument, even if that person is your best friend.

Alfred's mother came out of the kitchen just then and stood next to us. "There's just a lot you don't understand about the business world, Alfred," she said. "You're young, you're full of ideals, but things work slowly when there's a lot of money involved. I know that sounds terrible, but . . . it happens."

Mr. Caro gulped at his drink. "Is that pizza hot yet?" he asked angrily. Mrs. C. turned and went back into the kitchen.

"Yes . . ." she called. "The cardboard is steaming, it must be ready."

"Libby, did you put them in the oven in the *boxes*?" Mr. C. yelled.

"I know, Cray, I know I shouldn't do that, but I

don't have large trays and anyway, I don't leave it in that long and the oven isn't very hot."

"Get large trays, then, Lib," Mr. C. said. "I don't want cardboard in the oven."

"Okay, okay," she said and came in with the boxes, which she opened on the side table. "Cray?"

"What?"

"There's nothing on this pizza."

I went over and peered into the box she had opened. "No mushrooms," I said.

Alfred came over. "No pepperoni," he said.

"No sausage," Mrs. C. said.

I decided to brighten the mood. "But it sure looks like double cheese," I said.

Mr. Caro was rubbing his forehead. "Sorry," he mumbled. "Sorry. I was so distracted I don't even remember what I ordered. Can you all eat it with just the plain cheese?"

"Oh, sure!" I said.

Mrs. C. said, "Of course."

Alfred didn't say anything, I remember. I also remember that he didn't eat anything. And Mr. C. didn't eat much either. I did, though. I get real hungry when I'm upset. (Also, when I'm *not* upset.)

When I was through eating and when Alfred was through *pretending* he was through eating, he pulled me into the den.

"Listen, Rudy, we're not finished with this. It can't be dropped," he whispered. "Can it?"

80

I shook my head.

"Look, it's time for us to take over. Now when you come to school tomorrow, here's what I want you to bring. . . ." He got a pencil and paper and wrote it all down. Next he called Gillian and gave her almost the same instructions.

# 11

■ ■ ■ ■ ■ ■

"I got what you wanted, Alfred," I told him the next morning. I was bleary-eyed. "You know I was up till after eleven getting this stuff?"

"You're always up till after eleven, watching the late movie," Alfred said.

"Well, I don't get tired watching movies. It's work that makes me tired. Here." I took out a long sheet of yellow legal paper and handed it to Alfred.

"This's the list: every consumer agency I could find in the yellow pages and also what I was able to get from my father. You know, he didn't even ask me what I wanted it for? He was just glad I was doing something besides watching TV."

"I wish my brother would do something besides watch TV," Alfred said, studying the list. "Yeah, this looks good. Where's Gillian, have you seen her? I asked her to do the white pages, and I figured we'd all coordinate them together."

"No. Didn't she call for you this morning?" I asked. "As usual?"

"Gillian doesn't call for me *every* morning," Alfred answered. "She's only been doing it lately because we're both concerned about this whole thing."

"I'll bet," I said.

But just then, Gillian came running up to us. "Oh," she said, trying to catch her breath. "I really thought I was going to be late! My mother's alarm didn't go off, and we both overslept." She rummaged around in her big squashy shoulder bag. "Here, Alfred. I got every one I could find written right here. What do we do now?"

"During school I'll go over both your lists and get rid of any duplications we have. Then right after school, we go back to my house and start making phone calls."

By the time school was over, Alfred had coordinated our lists of consumer organizations. Each of us had listed all the departments under their general headings, and Alfred crossed off the ones that didn't seem to apply to "harmful food" and "toys." Many of the names on the list were *so* general, Alfred didn't know *what* they dealt with. He figured they'd just have to phone to find out.

Doreen and Douglas were home when we arrived, so we decided to use his parents' bedroom phone so they wouldn't be disturbed.

The first number was the *American Consumer Guide*, 555-5669.

"Sounds like a magazine," I said while Alfred dialed.

"Maybe it is," Gillian said.

"Shhh, it's ringing," Alfred said. "Hello? . . . *American Consumer Guide*? My name is Alfred Caro. I'd like to report a harmful product that's just hit the market. . . . Oh, you are? . . . Well . . . sure, okay. Alfred Caro, 555-3427." He hung up.

"What happened?" I asked.

"It was the answering service," he answered. "They're only in the office on Tuesdays and Wednesdays. She took my number."

"Well, let's go on," Gillian said.

So Alfred dialed the next one, Buyer Beware.

"Hello, is this Buyer Beware or the answering service?" he asked. "Oh . . . Well, yes, I have this harmful product to report . . . Okay, it's Alfred Caro, C-a-r-o, 555-3427."

84

"Answering service?" I asked. Alfred nodded. "Where *is* everybody?"

Alfred shrugged. "I don't know. How can they help if they don't go to work?"

Gillian said, "Well, let's forget it. Just try the next one."

"What is it?" Alfred asked.

"Concern for Consumers," I said, reading from the list.

"That sounds good. What's the number?"

I read, "555-7171," and Alfred dialed.

"Hello? My name is Alfred Caro and—Oh, jeez."

"What?"

"Somebody just said, 'One moment, please' and put me on 'hold.' "

"Oh, wow, this is going nowhere," Gillian moaned.

Alfred refused to be discouraged. "I'll wait just a minute," he said. Then, "Hello? . . . I'd like to talk to someone about a harmful product I discovered . . . Uh, no, it's not a food, but little kids might eat it. See, what it is, it's a ceramic mug . . . I'm twelve, why? . . . They'll be in tomorrow? Look, I don't understand. How come you people don't go to work every day? . . . Oh. Well, okay, but don't you want to take—" Alfred looked at us. "She hung up," he said. "She didn't even take my name and phone number, like the other two. I think she lost interest when I said I was twelve."

"What'd she say when you asked how come nobody's ever there?" I wanted to know.

"She laughed. She said they'd love to go to work everyday, but they didn't have the funds."

"Next!" Gillian called. She sounded like a drill sergeant.

So we marched on. We talked to groups like M.A.S.H. (Mothers Aim for Safe Households), the Public Interest Research Group, Household Products Research, Consumer Protection, Safe Toys for Our Children. A whole lot weren't there. Some took down Alfred's name and phone number and a bunch of information. A lot of them turned right off as soon as Alfred had to mention his age. One lady called Alfred "little boy," and *he* hung up on that one.

"Let's watch television," I muttered finally.

"Let's flunk out of school," Gillian sang at me.

"Ouch," I said. "Okay, what now?"

"We're not giving up," Alfred said. "We'll find someone who'll give us immediate action."

"Yeah," I said, holding up the list. "There are about forty more numbers on here. I should've brought my toothbrush. We'll be here all night."

"I'm losing my voice, Rudy," Alfred said, rubbing his throat. "You make some calls now. You know what to say."

"Yeah, I know what to say. 'I'm *not* a little boy, I'm *not* a little boy,' " I mimicked.

"Did we call the Better Business Bureau?" Gillian asked, looking at the list.

I yawned. "I don't think so. We thought they were too general."

Gillian sighed. "Let's try them. Maybe they'll give us some other numbers."

"We don't need more numbers," I groaned, but Gillian was looking up the number and Alfred was handing me the phone.

"Oh, all right." I dialed. "Better Business Bureau? Yeah, well, my name is . . . uh . . . Alfred Caro . . ."

"You can give your *own* name, Rudy," Alfred whispered, making a face.

"I mean, Rudy Sugarman," I said. She must have thought I was weird, but she didn't hang up. I went on. "I'd like to know if you can help me concerning this harmful product Alfred discovered. *I* discovered. Well, never mind who discovered it . . ."

"Rudy . . ." Alfred sighed.

"Okay," I continued. "Are you still there?"

"I'm here," the lady said. She sounded a little annoyed, so I figured I'd better fix it up.

"It really *is* harmful, ma'am," I said, trying to sound as grown up as I possibly could. "See it's this mug . . ." and I explained it in about three sentences. Alfred was nodding so I knew I did all right.

"Well, sonny," she said, and I made a face and shook my head at Alfred, "I think you'd better call

Product Safety, and here's the number," which she gave me. I hung up.

"She said to call Product Safety," I told Alfred, "and she called me 'sonny.' "

Alfred pointed to the phone. "Call Product Safety," he said.

I did and got a nice receptionist who really talked to me. She asked my name and all about the product and said she'd connect me with someone.

"Hey," I said to her, "how come you talked to me for such a long time without calling me 'little boy' or something?"

"I'm eighteen," she laughed. "I don't like to be treated like a kid, either!"

I wanted to ask her what she was doing tomorrow night after work, but she had already connected me with another extension. It rang, a man picked it up, and said his name, which I didn't get at all. I told him the story again.

"Well," he said when I'd finished, "you say the cartoon picture faded from the outside of the mug after the washing?"

"Yes . . ."

"No cartoon on the inside?" he asked.

"No . . ."

"All right," he said, and then he began to ask questions: a description of the mug; the date we noticed the fading; the manufacturer's name, which we couldn't find so we mentioned about the commercial for Allbright Foods; if there was an injury as a result of using the product; if it had been damaged first—stuff like that. Then when he asked for a "detail of the complaint," and I explained about the glaze inside getting into the drinks and all, he said, "*Inside*?"

"Yeah."

"Oh, well, that's not our department. You'll have to call the Food and Drug people."

"Wait a minute," I said. "What—?"

"You see, we handle drinking receptacles from the lip down on the outside. Once you get into something that affects food, that's the Food and Drug Administration. They cover the receptacle from the lip down on the *inside*."

I scratched my head. "Outside it's you, inside it's them?" I asked.

"Right," he said.

I started to tell him that the outside was also involved, and maybe he should consider working together with the Food and Drug Administration, but he was already giving me their number, and besides, I was confused enough as it was. I thanked him and hung up.

"Gillian," I said, "you want to do this one?"

"Uh-uh," she said.

"Alfred?"

"My throat hurts, Rudy," he said. "You do it. You're doing fine."

I sighed and dialed. I got another man whose name I couldn't understand when he said it, and he asked a whole bunch of questions similar to the guy from Product Safety. Then he said, "Okay, Rudy, we'll have someone over there in a couple of days to pick up your sample."

I put my hand over the mouthpiece. "He's going to send someone over here in a few days to pick up the sample," I told Alfred.

"Tell him he can get it on the shelves," Alfred said.

"You can get it on the shelves," I said.

"We will, but we want your sample, too," was his answer.

I told Alfred, who said, "Fine. Ask him how long it will take."

He explained that there was a routine that they went through, having the thing analyzed, investigating the manufacturer, and all, and he said they were real busy right now with the Christmas rush for toys. He said fall was always overloaded, and there never was enough staff to cover all the complaints immediately. There were priorities.

But at least he listened. At least he seemed interested, which was what I told Alfred after I hung up.

"Yeah, Rudy, but . . ."

Gillian said, "But what?"

"I don't want this thing to get lost in someone's

paperwork. I know they're busy but I want action *now*!"

Amen, I thought.

"Let's keep calling," Alfred said. "Your turn, Gilly."

She winced. "I'm not good at calling, Alfred," she protested.

"You will be after the first hundred," I told her, and flopped down on the floor.

"No going to sleep, Rudy," she said.

"Awww . . ."

Finally it was almost dinner time. "I'll never make it home," I said. "I'm wiped out."

"The night air will wake you up," Alfred said. "Besides, I need to be alone. I have to think."

"Okay," I said, but my eyes were closed, and I didn't move.

Alfred threw my jacket over my face. " 'Bye, Rudy!" he said, laughing. " 'Bye, Gillian. And by the way, you guys were really great. Thanks a lot."

"Thanks, pal," I told him.

"I didn't mean to push you around or anything, Rudy. It's just that this thing has me really bugged. And we're not giving up!"

"We can't," I informed him. "My conference is next week. Exactly five days from now."

The four Caros were in the middle of dinner when the phone rang that night. It was me.

"Alfred, I got this idea. Remember the guy who gave that lecture last week on environmental protection?"

"Yeah . . ."

"Well, how about calling *him*? You know, instead of all those faceless organizations and their hang-ups about kids?"

"Well . . . he talked about pollution," Alfred said, "not about consumer protection."

"I know, but he probably knows someone who could help us. Then we'd have a real name of a real person to talk to instead of Miss How-Old-Are-You-Little-Boy? and Mr. Sometime-In-The-Near-Future."

"Hey, Rudy," Alfred cried into the phone, "that's a great idea! Nice going!"

"I'm a good assistant, huh?"

"The best! What's the guy's name?"

"Oh. Yeah. His name. Don't you know?"

"No, I don't remember."

"Me neither. He had a beard, though . . ."

"That's not enough," Alfred said.

"Guess not. Sorry, pal. It was just a thought."

"Wait a minute, his name shouldn't be hard to get. He did speak at the school. The school will have his name!"

"That's right!" I said. "R.B. would know it. Hey, Alfred, let me ask him, okay? Please? It'll look so good if I show an interest!"

"Sure, you can ask him" Alfred said. "It was your idea."

"Oh, thanks. He'll be so impressed. Fantastic! See you first thing tomorrow in the science lab, okay?"

"You better watch it, Rudy," Alfred kidded me. "You might not only stay in school, you might start doing *well* or something terrible like that!"

# *12*

■ ■ ■ ■ ■ ■

"His name is Lloyd McWhinney. Here's his number, I got that from the office." I handed Alfred a small piece of paper.

"Did you talk to Dr. Rittenhaus yet?" Alfred asked.

"Sure did. I was here at eight-thirty!"

"Wow, that must have been hard after staying up so late with the Late Show."

"I didn't watch the Late Show," I told him. "I went to bed early. Well . . . early for *me*."

"I don't know, Rudy," Alfred said. "You're changing. I can't even remember the last time you mentioned Mary Louise."

I shrugged. "Mary Louise? Who's she?"

Alfred grinned. "Who's *she*?"

"Well, did you happen to notice the new Home Economics teacher?" I said, grinning back. "About twenty-five years old with long blond hair and no wedding ring?"

"Jeez, Rudy," Alfred laughed.

"We should really learn to cook, Alfred."

We were assembled in the Caro kitchen again at 3:30. Gillian and I watched while Alfred dialed. And we waited.

"Hello?" Alfred said. "Is this Lloyd McWhinney?" He listened, then covered the mouthpiece. "It's *him*," he whispered. "It's really him. A real person!" Then he went back to the phone: "Mr. McWhinney, my name is Alfred Caro, and I go to Briarfield. You lectured there last week, remember?" Then back to us: "He remembers!"

"Well, of course," Gillian said. "In fact, if he *didn't* remember, you should hang up!"

"Shh!" Alfred said and began his story. He started at the very beginning, from the arrival of the Sandalwood Sam mug right down to the frustrations from the organizations. "And then my friend Rudy remembered you and your talk, and we figured you'd probably know someone who could help us."

"Well, Albert—" Lloyd McWhinney began.

"Alfred," Alfred said.

"I'm sorry, *Alfred*," McWhinney said quickly. "You've called the right person! I know an organization that is just sitting around, even as we speak, *waiting* for your information."

"You do?" Alfred said, sounding happy. He made his thumb and forefinger into a circle and held it up with a grin for Gillian and me. "What's its name?"

"Okay, it's called Help Our Children Grow," McWhinney said next. "It's brand new, and it's made up of people not too much older than yourself. They're mostly high-school and college kids. Very bright, very concerned, all volunteers. They don't have an office, they work out of the president's basement over on the West Side. It's a brownstone. Believe me, they're real hustlers. Yours is the kind of story they've been waiting for."

"Are they in the phone book?" Alfred asked.

"Not yet, they're too new. But I have the number. Most of them are friends of mine."

"Okay," Alfred said, picking up his pencil. "Let's have it."

Alfred wrote: 555-6048. "Thanks, Mr. McWhinney. Thanks a lot. What name should I ask for?"

"Francine Loraszowicz. She's the president."

"Francine, uh . . ."

"Lor-*az*-o-wits," McWhinney pronounced, "and good luck!"

Alfred held the phone away from his ear so we could hear. Gillian and I leaned in as it rang at the other end.

"Hello?" a male voice answered.

"Is this Help Our Children Grow?" Alfred asked.

"It sure is," the voice said. "Can I help you?"

"Uh, I'd like to talk to Francine Loraz—uh, Francine Lor—Lorzo . . ."

"Fran!" the voice on the other end yelled. "Phone!"

"Coming!" we heard.

"It's a business call," the male voice whispered as someone took the phone.

"Help Our Children Grow, Fran Loraszowicz," said a female voice.

"Miss Lor . . . Lazor . . ."

"Call me Fran."

Alfred sighed. "Okay. I got your name from Lloyd McWhinney, uh, Fran. My name is Alfred Caro, C-a-r-o, and if you have a minute, I have a story!" He went through it again while Gillian stretched and I poured us all some milk.

We watched as Alfred spoke, repeating some things slowly, spelling "Sandalwood," "Choco-Rich" and "Bodeen." After a while, he listened, bubbled "thanks," gave his address and phone number, and hung up.

"Let's hear it," Gillian said. "What are they going to do?"

"They're going to tell the public the whole story," Alfred announced triumphantly. "Fran says that this kind of thing can be hushed up to protect big business. But if word gets out to the press . . ."

"And TV?" I asked excitedly.

Alfred nodded. ". . . and TV and everything, then people really sit up and take notice. She's coming right over."

"What for?" Gillian wanted to know.

"She wants to see everything. The mug, the stuff we wrote out . . . Everything. Then she's going to take it back to her place, and they're going to have a meeting about it. Come on, we've got work to do."

"What?" I wailed. "What work?"

"Ah, that's more like the old Rudy," Alfred laughed. "We've got to make two more copies of the experiments. You have one and I have one, but Gillian needs one and now Fran. So let's start writing."

Francine Loraszowicz arrived at the Caro apartment at 5:30.

"Wow," Alfred said without thinking.

She laughed. "I know, you're thinking I look young, right?"

"Yeah!" Gillian said and laughed herself. "You're my height . . . and weight, I bet."

"Well, honey, I'm twenty years old. I may be small . . . but I'm loud!"

98

"Good," Alfred said. "Let me show you the stuff."

After Francine had examined the three experiments, we all went into the kitchen, and Alfred took the mug down from the refrigerator and showed her how faint the design was. She watched and shook her head.

"That's heavy, Al," she said. "We're gonna pull out all the stops on this one. Tell your parents not to get scared if the newspapers start calling!"

"Really?" I cried.

"What're you gonna do?" Gillian asked.

"We have some good contacts on the *New York Post*, and Orvy knows someone on Channel Five News."

Gillian said, "Orvy?"

"He's in the group. You'll meet him." She took a card out of her purse and handed it to Alfred. "Be at my place tomorrow night at six-thirty." She turned to Gillian and me. "You, too," she said. "Meanwhile, let me have a jar of testing solution from the mug."

"What for?" Alfred asked.

"You'll see," Francine answered.

Gillian frowned, "Alfred, can your mother or father go with us tomorrow night?" she asked. "My mother'll never let me out at night without an adult. And she goes out Saturday nights with her boyfriend."

"Yeah." I knew I'd have trouble with that, too.

"I don't want to involve my parents in this now,"

Alfred said. "I really bugged my father, right from the beginning, and I don't want to bug him anymore. Besides, he didn't *do* anything, and I don't know what he'll say about what *we're* doing. It might hurt his feelings, or it might make him mad . . ."

Francine looked perplexed. "Gee, I'm sorry for the problem," she said, "but a lot of us have jobs on Saturdays." She made clicking noises with her tongue. "Let's see . . . *some* of us could be there in the early afternoon . . ." She shook her head firmly. "No. I want *everybody* to meet you, Al, and hear your story. This thing is really going to get Help-Grow off the ground! What a promotion!"

"You sound like an advertising agency," Alfred grumbled.

"Aw, wait a minute, Al," Francine said, putting an arm around his shoulder. "You have to realize something: selling is selling, it's the same no matter what the product is. Right now, *you're* the product—that is, your idea is. And *we're* your agency. We have to sell your idea to the people. Because without publicity, where would we be?"

"Just where I got," Alfred said. "Nowhere."

"That's why you came to us," Francine told him. "It's a question of values. Which product is more important. We think yours is. But selling is still selling. And in order to sell you need clout."

Clout, I thought. Oh, boy.

After Francine left, we had to figure out what to do about getting out at night without an adult. Adults! You can't get anywhere with them, and you can't get anywhere without them!

We were nowhere at all, when Doreen's high-pitched scolding voice came from the den: "Douglas, no! The last time we played 'The Creeping Fang' I had your teeth marks on my wrist for three days!"

Gillian and Alfred and I all looked at each other with the same thought.

"Doreen!" Alfred yelled, getting to the den first.

"What?" She and Dougy were watching "Woody Woodpecker." Doug was removing some plastic fangs from his upper teeth.

"What are you doing tomorrow night?" Alfred asked.

"Why, Alfred," Doreen smiled, "I didn't know you cared."

Alfred turned bright red.

"He's not asking you for a date, Doreen," Gillian giggled. "He wants to know if you could take us somewhere. To a meeting. We can't go out at night by ourselves."

Alfred was still red, so I explained about Help Our Children Grow.

"If you came with us, our parents would let us go," Gillian said.

"Yeah, okay, I guess I could," Doreen said. "I

just happen to be free tomorrow night. But you know what I get an hour for babysitting, Al."

Alfred's jaw dropped. *"Babysitting!"* he cried. "We're not *babies*, Doreen. We're performing a public service!"

*"You* may be performing a public service," Doreen said, "but while you're doing it, *I'm* babysitting."

"I'll chip in, Alfred," Gillian offered. "And so will Rudy."

"Listen, Gillian—" (They both glared at me, so I didn't finish.)

"Where are we going?" Doreen wanted to know.

Alfred looked at the card he was still holding. "The West Side," he told her. "West Seventieth Street."

"How do we get there?" Doreen asked. "Taxi?"

"Taxi! You're crazy!" Alfred said.

"Bus, then," Doreen said. "I get my fare paid."

"Boy, Doreen."

"What time?"

"Well, we have to be there at six-thirty," Gillian said, "so we probably have to leave here around six."

"Quarter-to," Alfred said, ". . . to be on the safe side. We'll have to pick up Rudy."

"What'll we tell our parents?" Gillian asked.

Alfred frowned. "I don't know," he said, rubbing his cheek. "I hate to lie, but I really want to keep them out of it."

102

"I know!" Gillian cried. "Let's tell them we're going out on a date. You and I! We'll say we're doubling with Doreen and her boyfriend. We'll say we're going to the movies!"

"Her boyfriend! That's me!" I cried.

"Just wait a minute," Doreen said.

I grinned at her.

"A double date with *twelve*-year-olds?"

Gillian sighed. "It's just pretend, Doreen. That's just what we'll tell our parents. We don't want them to know about the meeting."

Doreen said, "Well . . ."

"Good," Alfred said. "Then from here we'll go pick up Rudy. Our parents won't see him, so they won't know *he's* Doreen's date."

"Then it *is* a double date," Gillian said, smiling. "Doreen and Rudy and you and I."

I smiled at Gillian, but she wasn't looking at me.

# *13*

∎ ∎ ∎ ∎ ∎ ∎

Francine's house turned out to be one of those tall brownstones right near Central Park. She greeted us at the door wearing jeans and a black turtleneck, which bugged me because I had put on a checked sport jacket for the occasion.

We could hear some voices coming from somewhere in the house, like party-type noise—laughing and talking—and Doreen nudged Alfred and said, "What's going on?"

"Come on down," Francine said, smiling, "and find out." She led us to what turned out to be the basement stairs.

There was a nice-looking room down there with couches and a bunch of pillows on the floor and posters on the walls and about eight or nine people whose ages I'd estimate to be from eighteen to twenty-two. Everyone had on jeans except for one terrific-looking girl who had on a long dress with flowers all over it. They all looked up as we came down the stairs.

"Here they are!" Francine announced. "This one's Alfred and these are his assistants, Gillian and Rudy. And this is, uh . . ."

"This is Doreen," Alfred said quickly. "She brought us."

Doreen looked around the room and smiled. I could see why. It was like we had taken her to a party. And not one for twelve-year-olds.

Everyone said "hi's" and "hello's." Then one by one, they introduced themselves.

"Hi," Alfred said shyly when they'd finished.

"Okay," Fran said, still standing. "Does anyone have any questions he'd like to ask Alfred?"

"Yeah." One of the guys raised his hand. "How long has this promotion piece been on the market?"

"The first commercial was on last Saturday," Alfred told them.

"Allbright Foods, right?" I think it was Orvy. Alfred nodded.

A girl called Han Su raised her hand, and Francine pointed to her. "I ran the tests myself this afternoon, Alfred. You were right. You did a good job."

"Han Su works at a hospital," Francine explained. "In the pathology lab."

"There is a terrific concentration of lead in the glaze," Han Su said. "Inside and out. It really is dangerous."

"That's what *I* figured," Alfred said.

"I ran the same tests on some other receptacles," Han Su went on, "and didn't get a reaction, but when I made some more sophisticated experiments, I did find a small concentration of lead."

"Why is this particular one so high?" another girl wanted to know. Han Su frowned. "The glaze is faulty. That's what made the design fade in the first place."

"Well, what we've got here is something to make a scene about," another guy said. "And we've got to move fast. What's out there has to be recalled!"

"Right!" Alfred cried. Then Orvy spoke up. "I think we should tell them, Fran," he said.

"What?" Alfred asked.

"We have a surprise for you," Francine said, grinning. "*You* tell them, Orvy, it's your baby."

"Well . . ." Orvy began. He glanced at Francine, and both of them were beaming. "How'd you guys like to be on television?"

"What?" Alfred said.

"I said . . . How'd you like to be on television? *Tonight*!"

Was he kidding? On television? Me? Rudy M. Sugarman, son of Robert and Marjorie Sugarman of Manhattan? I started to shake. My whole dream come true! "A Word from Our Sponsor," starring Alfred Caro, co-starring Rudy—

"What do you mean, on television?" Alfred was asking. He didn't sound as thrilled as I was.

"See, I've got a friend at Channel Five News," Orvy explained. "I worked there last summer in the mail room. I'm a journalism major, and I want to be a—"

"Just *tell* them, Orvy!" someone yelled.

"My friend's name is Janice Pepper," Orvy went on. "And she's on her way over here to interview you kids. What do you think of that?"

Gillian said, "Wow!"

I was glad I had worn that plaid jacket! "Hey, do we need makeup or anything?" I asked.

"Listen to that, he's a natural-born star," said the girl in the long dress.

"There's a switch," Gillian said to me. "*On* the tube instead of *at* it."

"And it'll be on tonight?" Alfred asked. I thought he looked a little green.

"I'd bet," Orvy said.

"Are you okay, Alfred?" Francine asked.

He nodded. "Sure, I'm fine . . ." he told her.

"Don't be nervous, Alfred," said a girl called Melinda. "I did a commercial once. It's not bad in front of the camera. Only a little, in the beginning, but you get used to it real fast."

"That's the reason Melinda joined our group," Francine told Alfred. "The shampoo she used in the commercial gave her a head full of split ends."

"Alfred, are you sure you're all right?" Gillian whispered. "You look strange."

"Yeah . . ." he said. "Fran, can I use your phone?"

"My phone? Sure. Upstairs. In the kitchen. On your left."

I started to follow him, but I realized he wanted to be by himself. He almost tripped over Doreen as he headed up the stairs. I couldn't imagine why he wanted the phone, but I found out later, and it figured. It was just like Alfred.

He found the kitchen easily and the phone on the wall. He reached for it but drew back. Reached again, drew back.

"Take a deep breath," he told himself. He sniffed. "I won't stand here and cry. That won't get me anywhere. I have to call Dad, have to. Oh, but if I call him, he'll know I lied about going to the movies with Gillian. And then he'll find out what I *am* doing. But he has to know." And then he did a very un-Alfred-like thing. He slapped at the wall with his palm—hard—and hurt his hand. "He has to be here." He dialed his own number.

"Hello, Dad? This is Alfred. Listen, I think I'm in some trouble . . ."

Mr. Caro didn't get there before Janice Pepper and her film crew, but he did make it before any interviewing started. When he arrived at the Loras-zowicz doorstep, looking like the Ghost of Christmas-Yet-to-Come, the crew was busy adjusting their equipment and checking the lights and sound levels.

He started calling Alfred from the living room and continued until he was in the middle of the basement stairs. Alfred turned to look at him, and, boy, his face was white.

"Hi, Dad," he said with a small wave.

"Let's have it, young man. What's going on?"

Alfred came over to him. "I told you on the phone, Dad. I thought it was just going to be a meeting. You know, a consumer group meeting? That's all, I swear, I mean it. But when she told me that we were being interviewed on TV, I figured I better get you over here."

"You figured right. What about going to the movies? That's what you told us." Mr. Caro seemed to be grinding his teeth.

"Uh . . . Well, I *am* with Gillian . . . and Doreen . . ." Alfred pointed. "Rudy's here, too . . ."

I nodded and tried to smile.

"But not at the movies. That was a lie," Mr. Caro said.

"Dad, I didn't mean to lie. I just figured, you know, I'd nagged you so much, that from now on, we'd just leave you out of it. You know . . ."

Doreen came over. "Hi, Mr. Caro," she said.

Alfred said, "Listen, Doreen, thanks a lot for bringing us. How much do I owe you?"

I reached in my pocket for my share of the tab. But Doreen looked upset. "Look, you guys," she said, glancing around the room. "I . . . uh . . . I'd kind of like to stay, if that's okay . . . You . . . you don't have to pay me."

I smiled at her. "Ah, Doreen, I'm such a good date you don't want the evening to end, right?"

"Stifle it, Rudy," she said.

"Alfred!" someone yelled. "Ms. Pepper needs some levels, can you come on over here?"

"I didn't lie all the way, Dad," Alfred said pleadingly. "When it turned out this way . . . I called you . . ."

Mr. Caro tightened his lips. "Maybe you'd just better get your coat and come on out of here," he said.

"Alfred!" the voice called again.

"I can't," Alfred told him. "I couldn't now, even if I wanted to. And I don't want to, Dad, don't you see? It's important!" We both watched Mr. Caro's face, but I couldn't get a reading.

Finally, he said, "All right."

The basement, which had looked bright and

cheery to me when we first got there, had suddenly been transformed into Oz. It was weird. I'd never seen so much light. When the man in charge turned them on, it was so bright it hurt your eyes. And some of the lights were flickering on and off . . . it was unreal.

They put Alfred on a chair with Janice Pepper on one side of him and me on the other. Gillian was next to me and Francine was standing behind us.

Janice Pepper was wearing a tweed suit, and she smelled strongly of perfume. Her hair was pulled back tightly in what my mother calls a French knot; she reminded me of Joan Crawford in "Mildred Pierce." The cameraman held a portable camera aimed at us, and Pepper was saying, "Testing, one, two, three, four . . . Got my level? Let me give you my opening line, and you can get it from this: I'm here at the Headquarters of the Help Our . . ."

While she was talking, I got up and leaned way over so I could look into the lens of the camera. A camera. On *me*, Rudy M. Sugarman. I started to smile, and I guess I kind of got lost in the excitement because the next thing I knew Janice Pepper was saying, "Okay, hold it, none of that now . . ."

I said, "Huh?" It was like coming out of a dream.

"I can't have you bobbing and weaving behind me when I'm talking, son. What's your name again?"

"Rudy."

"Rudy. Right. I want you to be as natural as possible, so just sit still and be yourself, all right, Rodney?"

"Rudy!" (This was my first break. She *had* to get my name right!)

"Rudy. Sorry. Joe, were you able to get anything there? How's it look?"

The sound man said, "Okay here, Jan."

"Good. Now listen everybody . . ." The noise in the room died down as Janice Pepper raised her voice to include everyone. All of us turned to her. "As the camera pans the room, try not to look directly into the lens. Try not to look into the camera, have you got that? Just look at me. You'll be more relaxed, okay? Good. Now, you ready to roll, Fred?"

"Yeah," Fred said.

"Okay, roll . . ." Her face suddenly broke into a wide, bright smile. I wanted to laugh because she hadn't smiled once until the camera started rolling.

"I'm here at the Headquarters of Help Our Children Grow," she said. "These are young people, volunteers all, who are simply dedicated, concerned—"

"Hold it, Jan," the cameraman interrupted. "The kid's head is blocking the light. Kid, can you move a little to the left?"

Alfred looked up, startled. "Who, me?" he mouthed. The cameraman nodded and waved his hand to where he wanted Alfred to move.

112

"Right. Good. Okay, Jan."

"Can you pick up some of these kids' faces, Fred?" Pepper asked.

"Oh sure, no problem. I'm rolling." And Fred began moving the camera from one face to another. I found it hard not to look at the camera, like Janice Pepper had said, and I don't know what my face was doing, but I tried to stare so hard at her instead of at that lens that I thought I was dissecting every pore of her skin.

"These are young people," Pepper began again, "all volunteers. Young people vitally concerned with our safety and health, and by that I mean, *yours* and *mine*. They've come to me with a story that deserves as much publicity as it can get." With her right arm, Pepper motioned to Francine, while she continued to smile directly at the camera. "This is the group's president, Ms. Francine Loraszo-wicz—" (Francine smiled nervously) "—and just yesterday, she received a telephone call from a very special young man, sitting here on my right." I saw the camera turn in Alfred's direction. "Tell us your name," Pepper said kindly, touching Alfred's hand.

"Uh, Alfred Caro."

"And how old are you, Alfred?"

"Twelve."

"And tell us, Ms. Loraszowicz, what did Alfred say to you on the phone?" She held her microphone up to Francine.

"Well," Francine began, "he—"

"Cut," from the cameraman. "Can you move in a little closer, honey?" to Francine. "Fine. Okay, pick it up."

"Uh, well, Alfred said that his father," Francine looked over at Mr. Caro, who was leaning forward in a chair, "who works for a big advertising agency, had given his younger brother a drinking mug with a picture on it. A cartoon. And Alfred noticed that after he put the mug through the dishwasher, the color on it faded."

Janice leaned her microphone in Alfred's direction. "And then what, Alfred?" she asked, smiling the whole time.

"Well, see, my friends—" Alfred began, but was stopped by some frantic motions from the sound man. Alfred nodded. He took a deep breath. "My friends and I," he said loudly, "here they are— Rudy Sugarman and Gillian Tenser—we, uh, tested the mug. To find out what was in the color. We did several tests—" Alfred stopped and looked at me. He dipped his head a little. "Uh, you want to tell what we found, Rudy?" he asked.

I thought: That's my friend Alfred for you. Giving me the credit—letting me talk on TV! Janice Pepper put the microphone in front of my face. I cleared my throat. "We found . . ." I paused (you know, to build up the suspense) ". . . *lead*. Lead in the glaze."

She took the microphone away from me and stuck

it back in Alfred's face. "An unusual concentration of lead, wasn't it?" Still smiling.

"Yes it was. Right, Gillian?" Alfred said. I saw her smile and I smiled, too, because now Janice Pepper had to talk to Gillian whether she wanted to or not.

She leaned the microphone toward Gilly.

"Yes. It was very high," Gillian said. She sounded shy.

Whoosh! The mike went from Gilly and back toward Alfred. Alfred nodded at Han Su, sitting on the floor. "One of the people in this group tested it in a lab, and she said that. That it was a very high concentration." The camera moved around until it found Han Su, then came back to Alfred.

"And what did you do when you found the lead?" Pepper asked.

"I told my father about it," Alfred said softly. The sound man held his hand cupped to his ear and motioned again. "I told my *father* about it," Alfred said, louder.

"Your father's advertising agency was responsible for the promotion, right?"

"Right."

"And what did your father do?"

Alfred looked over at his father, who was watching, his face a blank.

"He . . . he tried to tell someone, but, uh, they wouldn't listen. That is, they . . . they said that

115

companies make dishware like this with pictures and designs all the time and that they know what they're doing."

"In other words," Janice Pepper said, taking the microphone and turning toward the camera, ". . . 'You're just a kid, what do *you* know.' Right, Alfred?"

"Right," Alfred said.

Francine suddenly moved in toward the interviewer. "Alfred called a lot of people after that," she said, ignoring the frown from Pepper for speaking before she was spoken to, "and most of the people said the same thing—that he was just a kid. Or they brushed him off with talk of 'routine investigations.' But *we* listened. Help Our Children Grow listened! And took immediate action!" She stepped back.

"You certainly did," Janice Pepper said. "Now, hold up the mug, dear, won't you, so we can all see it?"

Francine held the mug while the camera zoomed in on Sandalwood Sam.

"This is the mug," Pepper said, her voice heard over the picture. "It's being seen in commercials for Choco-Rich Syrup, a product of Allbright Foods, Incorporated."

I saw Alfred try to look at his father out of the corner of his eye. I knew the camera wasn't on me so I turned my head to look, too. But Mr. Caro's expression was still totally blank.

116

The camera returned to a closeup of Janice Pepper's face. "Alfred's father happens to be here with us tonight . . ." She smiled. "And I know that we'd all like to hear from him." She turned to her left, and the camera followed. Mr. Caro was suddenly spotlighted.

"This is Mr.—" Pepper stopped, which was a cue for Mr. Caro to deliver his first name.

"Caro," he said.

Janice Pepper gave a soft laugh. "Yes, I know," she said. "I meant your *first* name."

"Creighton."

"Mr. Creighton Caro," she continued. "Tell us, Mr. Caro, what do you think of this son of yours? Under normal circumstances, I assume you'd be very proud. But in light of the fact that your agency was responsible for the product—"

Mr. C. coughed, reached for something in his pocket, changed his mind. "Well, we weren't responsible for the product, just the promotion."

"But when Alfred came to you with the evidence that it was not only a defective product, but actually a dangerous one, what did you do?"

"I tried . . . to reach the . . . I presented Alfred's findings to some of the members of the agency, but they weren't as concerned as Alfred."

"Or as concerned as you?"

"I was concerned, yes," he said more firmly. "But I would have kept it a company matter. Alfred, on the other hand, is not involved in the company or company ways. He has always felt that commercials and advertisements should do exactly what they promise to do. Not that they *don't*, but you see, not everyone reads the same things into them."

Janice Pepper nodded, urging him to continue by keeping the microphone in front of his face.

Mr. Caro seemed to be looking down at his knees or his feet or something. I got the feeling he wasn't really listening to Janice Pepper, he was listening to something inside his own head. Like when you're coming to a decision. I've seen it in movies, where you can tell from their faces that people are about to come to some earth-shattering conclusion any second now, and you're watching the last stages of their thoughts: five, four, three, two, one, *thought*!

He suddenly looked up, not at Janice Pepper, but at the camera, and he scraped his upper lip with his lower front teeth for a moment before he spoke again. "Those with more sophisticated taste are able to remove the hard sell, and make a decision based on how valuable the product might actually be to them. Children, on the other hand, tend to believe it all. That's why Alfred became so attuned to honesty in products and in the people who make and sell them. Faulty toys, for example, always disturbed him." He looked directly at Alfred. "I'm proud of Alfred. I underestimated him. So did my company. Our mistake was thinking we knew more because we were adults. We didn't. I'm sure that Ditmar-

Krebs-Patten will be proud of Alfred, and I'm sure that Allbright Foods will be proud, too. Everyone needs a conscience to oversee his actions, and the business community can count itself lucky it has Alfred."

Alfred was pointing to us and saying, "And Rudy, too, and Gillian!" but no one heard him because the whole room broke into spontaneous applause as Janice Pepper said, "Janice Pepper at Help Our Children Grow, Three-six-oh West Seventieth Street in Manhattan. And now, back to our studio and, probably, a word from our sponsor."

"Did you get all the kids?" Janice Pepper asked the cameraman.

"Oh, yeah,"

"Okay, let's pack it."

"Come on now," the sound man said, "pack it up! Push it, push it!" And almost instantly the lights and the feeling of being in Oz were gone. Our big moment. All gone. Now the room seemed very dark and not cheery at all.

"Watch it tonight!" Janice Pepper yelled, flying up the stairs. "It's a beauty!"

Gillian said, "Whew!" and leaned against the wall.

Francine came over. "You kids were terrific," she said. "So were you, Mr. Caro. Stay and watch it with us. We've got some interesting refreshments."

"No. We'll go home," Alfred's father said.

Alfred picked up the mug from the floor where Francine had left it. "Okay, Gilly. Come on, Rudy. We're going home. Doreen?"

Doreen was sitting on the floor next to one of the Help Our Children Grow guys. They were real close together.

"It's okay, Al," the guy said. "I'll take Doreen home."

Doreen got up from the floor and went to Alfred. She bent down and whispered into his ear. Alfred smiled, and we began to follow his father up the stairs.

"What'd she say to you?" I whispered.

He turned around and cupped his hand over his mouth. "She said she'd double-date with us anytime," he said.

"Stay there!" Mr. Caro barked, once Francine's door had closed behind us. He walked to the edge of the sidewalk and looked up the street for a taxi. He caught an empty one coming down from Central Park West, hailed it, and waved to us on the steps.

"Get in," he said, holding the door open. Alfred, Gillian, and I got into the back, and Mr. Caro slipped into the front seat with the driver.

"What's your address, Rudy?"

I told him.

"Go there first," he said to the driver. "Then we're going four blocks north."

120

"Dad, you were really terrific," Alfred said. "Everything you said . . ."

"I meant what I said," Mr. C. replied and whirled around to face Alfred, "but I mean this, too. You lied to me about where you were going! You put me in an extremely awkward position—"

"But, Dad—"

"You let me finish!" His father pointed a finger. "I am very upset about this . . . and I'm going to be very careful in choosing the right punishment for you."

"Gee, Mr. Caro . . ." Gillian began. "Please don't be too mad at Alfred. He made everyone know about the lead in the paint. . . . He showed that kids can really have clout after all. He only said we were going to the movies because—"

"That's enough, Gillian. I know what he did and why he did it."

Alfred looked at Gillian quickly and then put his head down. The rest of the ride home was silent.

I got off at my place and barely said good night to Alfred. I was really nervous for him. Me, I'm used to trouble. I've been in and out of it all my life. But Alfred—he's a newcomer. So I worried about the rest of that ride home. I shouldn't have because it actually turned out okay. When they got home, naturally they had to wait for the slowest elevator in New York.

Alfred and his father rode with Gillian up to her

floor and took her to her apartment to make sure she got in safely, since her mother wouldn't be home for a while yet.

"She'll miss the program," Gillian said sadly.

Alfred said, "Call your father. Will he be home?"

"Yeah, probably. He'll watch it. 'Night, Alfred. 'Night, Mr. Caro. Thanks for seeing me home."

"'Night, Gilly," Alfred said. He and his father walked back to the elevator, which had moved on to another floor.

Mr. C. pressed the button again.

"Alfred?"

"Yes?"

"I want to apologize for blowing up at you in the cab. In front of your friends."

Alfred looked up. "I understand, Dad," he said.

"I was very angry."

"I know."

"You never should have lied to your mother and me."

Alfred shifted his feet. "I wouldn't have, if I'd known about what they were going to do . . ."

"That's no excuse. There's no excuse for lying. You've never done that before. We've always had an open relationship."

"Yeah . . ." Alfred said miserably. "I'm sorry." He rubbed the mug, wishing it were Aladdin's lamp. They waited again for the slowest elevator in New York.

122

Mrs. Caro was in the living room.

"What happened?" she asked, getting up from the couch.

"We're going to be stars," Mr. C. said. "We're on the news."

"They really had the news people there?"

"They really did," he said and hung up his coat.

"What time?" she asked.

"Ten o'clock," Alfred told her.

"'Bout half an hour," she said. "That gives us some time to talk to you, young man."

"Dad already talked to me," Alfred said. "I'm sorry I didn't tell you the truth about where we were going. I won't do that anymore."

"But Doreen was there with you? You didn't go alone?"

"No . . . Doreen was there. She's *still* there."

"What do you think, Cray?" she asked.

"I think I'll probably get fired," he said.


Would you believe it? From the minute Alfred and his father and Gillian dropped me off at my building, all I could think of was: Okay, parents, okay, Bob and Marjorie Sugarman, your baby boy is about to become a star! Wait till you see! And guess who was waiting there for me in my apartment in all her glory? Mrs. Fazenda. Our housekeeper. Hired by Bob and Marjorie Surgarman to wait for me and stay until they got home from their party. A party! On the night of their only child's television debut! Of course, they didn't *know* it was the night of their only child's television debut. . . .

So I fixed that. I called the number they had left with Mrs. Fazenda, and told them all about my evening's work.

I'd love to say they were thrilled. And I can! They were thrilled. At least my mother *sounded* thrilled. She said to heck with the dessert they were starting, they were just going to be rude to their hosts and go into another room to watch television. I told them they were chips off the old block and hung up.

And with minutes to spare. I poured myself a Hawaiian Punch and sat down to watch the Ten O'Clock News. Starring Rudy Sugarman! Well . . . no, not really, but we all have to start somewhere.

And then it was on. It began with the announcer's words, ". . . And now from West Seventieth Street, here's Janice Pepper" and ended with: ". . . back to our studio and, probably, a word from our sponsor," from Janice Pepper herself.

Naturally, the first thing I did when the program was over was try to call Alfred. I was kind of worried about him. After all, I had nothing but glory from this whole thing, but for Alfred . . . there was a little more to it. It never fails—when parents are involved in your daily doings, all they do is complicate matters.

Well, I tried to call. And tried. And tried. The line

was busy. I wondered what was going on. It took me until a quarter to twelve to get through, but I figured it was okay, since they had to be up.

Alfred answered the phone. "Hi, Rudy," he said. He sounded wiped out. "I'm really glad it's you. It's really gone bazooey over here."

"Yeah, who've you been on the phone with all this time?"

"You wouldn't believe it. The newspaper and the wire services have been ringing this phone off the wall."

"Wanting to talk to *you*?" I asked.

"Yeah . . . but that's not what the really bad thing is. . . ."

"What's the really bad thing?"

"Mr. Krebs called."

"Mr. Krebs, your father's boss?" I asked.

"Not anymore," Alfred said.

"Oh, no . . . "

"Yeah. He fired my father."

I couldn't believe it. "Listen, Alfred, how could he do that? He ought to be *grateful* to your father!"

"He wasn't very grateful." Alfred really sounded awful, and I didn't blame him. Poor Mr. Caro. Poor Alfred. Talk about unfair! "Hey, Rudy . . . I think I'd better hang up. I don't feel too well. . . ."

"Yeah, pal," I told him, "I know how you must feel. Boy, that's really rotten!"

"It's rotten all right, but I *really* don't feel very

well. I think I've got a temperature or something."

"Look, Alfred," I began. I wanted to say something that would help, but I just didn't know what. "I bet you're really okay, but just feeling lousy about your father. How about if you go to bed, get a good night's sleep, and give me a call tomorrow, okay?"

"Yeah," he said, "you're probably right. I'll call you tomorrow."

# 14

■■■■■

I spent Sunday hanging around waiting for Alfred to call. He didn't, but I did get some of the calls from the newspapers that he'd started to get the night before, and I must admit it was kind of fun, except I couldn't answer a lot of the technical science questions they asked me and I kept wishing Alfred were there to field those. I would've enjoyed all the attention a lot more if I hadn't been worried about Alfred and his family and wondering what was going on.

Finally, almost around dinner time, Gillian called.

"Alfred asked me to call you," she said. "He's exhausted from talking on the phone. I tried to call him all day but couldn't get through, so I finally went down there."

"Well, gee, I'm glad you called, Gilly," I told her. "Tell me what's going on."

"You wouldn't believe the calls—newspapers and everything . . ."

"Yeah, I got some myself," I said.

"Me, too, but Alfred was bombarded! And also Francine called—you know, from Help Our Children Grow? She said Alfred was a baby Ralph Nader, and she said she's got two speaking engagements lined up, interviews with the *Daily News* and the *New York Post*, and a 'possible' on 'The Johnny Carson Show'."

"A 'possible'?" I asked.

"Well, Orvy has this friend at the *Post* who has a sister who dates some guy whose second cousin works on the show out on the West Coast."

"Oh. Orvy sure has a lot of friends."

"Francine says we can't imagine what this has done for consumer advocacy. She says we really should be proud of ourselves."

"I'll be prouder if it keeps me in school," I said. And then I felt very guilty. Thinking of myself again, when poor old Alfred . . . "Look, Gilly, did Alfred tell you what happened to his father?"

"Oh, yeah! That's the best part! He's not fired!"

"He's *not*?"

"No! Mr. Krebs called him this morning and said he was 'overwrought' the night before."

"Overwrought?"

"That's what Alfred said his father said Mr. Krebs said. Anyway, Mr. Caro was called to a meeting at Ditmar-Krebs."

"Wait a minute, Gilly . . ." I was trying to sort out what she was saying. "You mean that when you got down to Alfred's, Mr. Caro wasn't there because he was at a meeting? On Sunday?"

"No, Rudy, Mr. Caro was there when I went to Alfred's. He was back from his meeting. He was lying down," she said.

"Well, what happened at the meeting?"

"They hired an investigative committee to look into it."

I sighed. "I thought *we* already did that," I said.

"No, it's more complicated, Rudy. Anyway, that's where they left it. They're 'looking into it.' "

"I don't get it, Gillian," I told her.

"Well, Rudy, maybe I got it wrong or I left out something or *Alfred* left out something, but that's all I know for now. Oh, yeah, except for one more thing . . . Don't look for Alfred in school tomorrow. He's got the chicken pox."

# *15*

■ ■ ■ ■ ■ ■

Well, that was yesterday and my conference is tomorrow, but I'm not worried anymore. No way. Especially after what happened today. I thought the story was really all over and I'd come out on the top rung of everyone's Good Will Ladder. Only it wasn't over. Completely.

After school, I decided to go see Alfred. I figured it'd be okay since his father hadn't been fired after all and since I'd already had the chicken pox. Anyway, I wanted to cheer him up—impress him with all the notes I took for my conference report. So I went over there again, right after school. Gillian came with me.

Mrs. Caro had stayed home from work to take care of Alfred and answer the phone calls which were still coming in. She was pretty exhausted, but not too exhausted to invite Gilly and me for dinner, which we both accepted happily.

Alfred was in bed in his room, a big blob of calamine lotion, whiter than his bedsheets.

"Your notes are great, Rudy," he said after he'd examined them. "Dr. Rittenhaus will be bowled over."

"He already is," I said. "I think my report will be icing on an already perfect cake. He saw us on TV."

"He *did*?" Alfred grinned.

"He sure did. He said to me, 'Well, Rudy, the worm certainly has turned.' "

"The worm?"

"Yeah. Sounds like something my father would say. And mean it as a compliment."

"Well, it *is* a compliment," Gillian said. "You really did a good job, Rudy."

I was surprised. "Thanks, Gilly," I said. "So did you."

Mrs. C. came into the room with Douglas trailing her. "Alfred, there's a man here to see you," she said.

"Me?" he asked.

She stepped aside and a real tall guy walked into the room. "Alfred?" he said. I pointed. "The one in the bed," I said.

"Hi, I'm Frank DeWitt from the Food and Drug Administration," he said.

Alfred said, "Hi."

"Well!" Mr. DeWitt said. "You gave us quite a busy weekend." He didn't sound too pleased.

Mrs. Caro motioned me from behind Mr. DeWitt to get up off the only chair in the room and I quickly jumped up. "Here, uh, sir," I said, offering the chair. "Sit down."

"Thank you. Now, Alfred, you spoke to Mr. Derounian in our office, didn't you?" he asked.

Alfred said, "Uh, I might have. Maybe Rudy did. Or Gillian. I don't remember the name. . . ." He dabbed his arm with cotton-soaked calamine.

Mr. DeWitt checked his notepad. "Yes, you called on Thursday afternoon. And Mr. Derounian told you we'd have someone come by and pick up a sample from you?"

"Yes . . ." Alfred said, "but we were so tired after all the phone calls, and it seemed like we were just getting the runaround. . . ."

Mr. DeWitt shook his head. "So you went on television." He looked at all of us, and we just nodded. "We weren't giving you kids the runaround," he said. "But there are procedures to be followed. And priorities."

132

"Priorities?" Alfred asked.

"For example, if a case of botulism were reported, we'd be flying into action in seconds! But there weren't any injuries reported from your mug yet, and there wouldn't be for a while. Not with this particular problem."

Alfred said, "But—"

"Look, Alfred . . ." Mr. DeWitt began, but Alfred held up his hand.

"These are my friends, Rudy and Gillian. We all worked on this," he said.

Mr. DeWitt nodded and included us. "See, kids, this mug might leach lead into your drinks, and over a period of time, it would be dangerous. But we have to make our own investigation first. If you were wrong in your findings, you would have panicked the public unnecessarily by going on television. And if everyone did that everytime they suspected something, we'd all be in trouble. Understand?"

Alfred nodded. "We thought we were being brushed off because we were kids," he said.

"I'm sure that happens many times," Mr. DeWitt said, and he smiled. "But not always. And you don't have to be a kid to be frustrated by calling government agencies."

"Or any organization, for that matter," Mrs. C. said, and they both laughed.

"Now, Alfred, may I have the sample?"

"Come with me, Mr. DeWitt," Mrs. Caro said. "I'll get it for you."

Mr. DeWitt stopped in the doorway and turned back to us. "Don't be afraid to call us," he said. "And next time, be sure to get the name of the person you're speaking to so you can follow up. But try to stay off the tube first, unless you sing, dance or tell jokes."

Quickly, I said, "Hey, Mr. DeWitt, have you heard the one about the—"

"Shut up, Rudy," Gillian said.

Alfred said, "I have *your* name now, Mr. De-Witt," and the man smiled.

After he had gone, Mrs. Caro came back into Alfred's room. "Guess what we're having for dinner tonight?" she said.

"Frozen fish sticks," Alfred said.

"Frozen pizza," Dougy offered.

I started to say, "Frozen—" but she cut me off.

"*Not* frozen. I'm not opening one fast food package tonight. We're having an entirely organic casserole."

Dougy said, "Yuck!"

"No additives, no artificial coloring, no monosodium glutamate . . ."

Alfred said, "No, BHA, no BHT . . ."

". . . No diglycerides, no monoglycerides . . ." his mother continued, "just plain old back-to-nature."

Gillian and Alfred applauded.

"Thank you, thank you," Mrs. C. said. "But if you hate it, I don't want to hear about it."

"We'll love it," Alfred said, "whether we do or not."

Douglas went to Alfred's bedside and handed him a plastic robot. "Alfred, can you fix my robot?" he asked.

"Say 'please,' " Mrs. C. said.

Douglas said, "Please."

Alfred looked at the robot and pressed a button on its shoulder. "The battery's dead, Dougy," he said, "That's all. Go get a transistor battery out of my drawer over there."

"Is that one of the ones shaped like a rectangle?" Douglas asked. Alfred nodded, and Doug brought it to him.

Alfred began to mess around with the toy. "What does it do when the battery's working?" he asked Douglas.

"His mouth lights up," Douglas answered.

"His *mouth*?" Alfred asked, staring at the robot. "His mouth *lights up*?"

"Uh huh," Douglas said. "He shoots a deadly dental ray and kills all his enemies."

Alfred looked at me and Gillian. "He couldn't have made that up," he said. "He's only six."

"*Hello!*" came a yell from the living room.

"It's your father!" Mrs. Caro said to Alfred.

"He's home so early!" She began to look worried.

"Your father, the king, has returned from battle," Dougy cried. "Make ready the feast."

"Oh, yeah," I said to Doug. " 'Prince Valiant.' "

"Right," he said.

Mrs. Caro started for Alfred's door, but Mr. C. came in first.

"Cray?" Mrs. Caro said, touching his arm. "Is anything wrong?"

"No, Lib, everything's okay." He smiled and sat down on the edge of Alfred's bed. Alfred told him about Mr. DeWitt's visit.

"Yeah," Mr. C. said, "I'm sure the FDA will make it's own investigation, but Allbright did one over the weekend. They had to, after that broadcast. . . . Anyway, the promotion's been shelved. . . ."

"We were right!" I cheered.

"Of course we were right," Alfred said.

"Yes," Mr. Caro said, "you were. Right after the story came out, Allbright sent an investigating committee over to the factory where the mugs are made. They've been working on it nonstop, and we got the report today. That's why I came home early, to tell you about it." He smiled. "And besides, they gave me the rest of the week off."

Mrs. C. said, "Really?"

"Yep. So you can go back to work tomorrow, Libby. I'll take care of the guys. Now, here's what the investigators found out about the mugs: You see, the factory made up its glaze formula, but they had to buy their components, their raw materials, from an outside source. They put in their order for the right formula, and they naturally assumed that that's what would be delivered. The formula they ordered."

"And it wasn't?" Alfred asked.

"It wasn't. The company producing the components made a mistake. There was a higher concentration of lead in the formula than the factory had ordered. But it was only one bad batch."

"And the mug we tested was from that batch?"

"That's right. And everyone is grateful that you found it before there was any real harm done."

"That's why Mr. Krebs fired you on Saturday night, huh?" Alfred said sarcastically.

"Now, wait a minute, Alfred. Naturally a corporation has a public image to maintain. When Mr. Krebs saw me on television, he had no idea of the circumstances. He just saw me up there, putting the company in what he considered a bad light. It wasn't the agency's fault the product was defective, and it doesn't help the agency's image to be exposed that way. Mr. Krebs wasn't exactly delighted with the exposure when he saw it on the news."

"Well, we wouldn't have *gone* on the news if Mr. Diedrickson had just paid attention to you in the first place," Alfred said.

"Uh, right," Mr. C. said. "That's what Mr. Krebs said, too."

"He did?"

"Yes. He fired Mr. Diedrickson."

"He *did*?" That was from me and Gillian and Alfred together.

"Yes, he did. He felt Mr. Diedrickson should have checked it out further. It was his account. . . ."

"Why *didn't* he?" Alfred asked.

Mr. C. winced. "Well, he was very involved, he had his commissions to think of, there was a lot of money on the line . . . and he kept saying you were only . . ."

"Twelve!" Alfred shrieked, and his father nodded.

"Well, Alfred proved that kids can have clout after all," Gillian said proudly. "I'll bet the next time your agency has a bad product they'll listen to Alfred, Mr. Caro."

Alfred's father groaned.

"I'm glad you didn't get fired, Dad," Alfred said. "but maybe you should think about quitting the ad business. All the rip-offs and all the hassles to get things fixed . . . Big Business just doesn't care about the little guy."

"Alfred, you're making it a black-and-white issue again with no room for gray. And don't make me your next crusade. I do care about the ads I write, and I'm good at my job. It rewards me by giving me financial security for myself and my family. I have a wonderful wife, two wonderful sons. . . ."

"Yay!" Dougy shouted.

138

". . . I'm a lucky man, and I think I'm doing what's right for *me*. *You* have to do what's right for *you*. That's how we have to lead our lives."

"Well, you stood by me, Dad, and I'm proud of you." Alfred said.

Mr. Caro looked like he was going to cry, but he didn't. He cleared his throat and said, "Thank you, son."

Mrs. Caro really worked hard on that organic casserole. What it was, was green, yellow, orange, and purple. That's all I can say about it, except after all that buildup between her and Alfred, I would've eaten it if it got up and ran around the plate. Alfred shoveled it all in with what looked like pleasure, but Gillian and I took it a little slower, kind of catching each other's eye with each forkful. Dougy just wouldn't eat it at all and got a big lecture from his brother about how his tastes had been ruined over the years.

But dessert was good. Jell-O with bananas. And afterward, I got up to go.

"I really want to thank you all, but I have to run now. My dad's meeting me downstairs."

"But it's early, Rudy," Alfred said.

"Well, pal—" I touched his shoulder. "Got a big day tomorrow."

"Right!" he cried. "Your conference! Well, there's nothing to worry about now."

"True," I said, "but I need my beauty sleep so I can appear in R.B.'s office typecast in the role of Rudy Sugarman, Dedicated Student."

"Good for you, Rudy," Mrs. Caro said.

"Hold it," Gillian said, getting up from the table. We all watched her as she went into the den, and just looked at each other until she came back out. She was holding a copy of *TV Guide*.

"What is it, Gilly?" Alfred asked.

"I just wanted to check out this new role of Rudy Sugarman, Dedicated Student."

"What do you mean?" I asked, beginning to smile.

Gillian smiled, too. "Are you going home for your beauty sleep?" she asked. "Or for 'Gunga Din,' with Cary Grant, Victor McLaglen, and Douglas Fairbanks Junior? It's going on at eight o'clock."

"I'm shocked!" I said, clutching my chest. "How could you possibly suggest that—"

"If you leave now, you can just make it," Mrs. C. said, looking at her watch.

" 'Bye!" I called, and was out the door.

## About the Author

Judie Angell has written four novels for young people: *Tina Gogo*; *Ronnie and Rosey*; *In Summertime It's Tuffy*; and *A Word From Our Sponsor* or *My Friend Alfred*. Before publishing her first children's book, in 1977, she taught elementary school, wrote promotion copy for Channel 13, New York City's educational television station, and did editorial work for *TV Guide*.

Judie Angell lives with her husband, a musician, and their two sons in a house on a lake in South Salem, New York.